RAWHIDE CREEK

RAWHIDE CREEK

L.P. HOLMES

A Black Horse Western

ROBERT HALE · LONDON

ISBN 0 7090 4905 6

Robert Hale Limited
Clerkenwell House
Clerkenwell Green
London EC1R 0HT

Photoset in North Wales by
Derek Doyle & Associates, Mold, Clwyd.
Printed and bound in Great Britain by
WBC Print Ltd, and WBC Bookbinders Ltd,
Bridgend, Mid-Glamorgan.

ONE

Stepping from the second coach of the narrow gauge combination freight and passenger train at Chinese Flat, Cleve Ellerson owned the clothes on his back, the big Colt gun shoved from sight under a frayed denim jumper, and something less than half a sack of Durham tobacco in the pocket of a faded calico shirt.

It had been a tiresome, all night ride and the last time he had tasted solid food was some twenty hours gone. Also, plaguing him, was the bite of weakness from the lately healed bullet wound across his ribs. His real destination, the booming placer gold camp of Rawhide Creek, was still long miles distant beyond the Carson summit, and with stage seats certain to be at a premium, prospects of a ride for anyone with pockets as empty as his, would surely be remote.

Chinese Flat was a rough and ready, end-of-track layout with its several raw-boarded buildings clustered about the corrals and feed sheds of a sprawling stage and freight compound. Two of the largest structures were freight warehouses. There was a stage station and another building combining a bar, an eating house and a hotel of sorts. A couple of big, double-hitch Merivale freight outfits stood ponderous, patient and empty by the warehouse and a stage was making up for the run

5

across the mountain.

Ellerson was not the only one to leave the train. a gambler in a wide black hat and long black coat was just ahead of him together with a rush of itinerant miners who gathered about the stage and argued for seats.

Up at the lead coach a brakeman offered a steadying hand to a final descending passenger. She came off the coach steps with a quick, easy grace, a slender figure in a long blue cloak and a sort of poke bonnet hat. The brakeman was pointing.

'That would be your stage making up yonder, Miss. If you're figuring on a seat you best get right over there.'

Her voice was low and pleasant as she thanked the brakie, and when she passed Ellerson he glimpsed thick chestnut hair caught back from a serene, warm-cheeked face. As he took his own forlorn hope over to the stage he saw her accost a harried man who had been selling seating space on a first come, first served basis. To the girl the agent shook a regretful head.

'Sorry, miss – just filled the last seat. You'll have to wait over for tomorrow's run.'

When she would have argued, the agent turned obdurate. 'Can't chance it miss. Last agent who overloaded a Scotty Duncan stage got fired, and me – I like my job.' He wheeled toward the compound and lifted an impatient yell. 'Come on, Boyle – look alive! Get that team out here!'

A burly man with a whiskey-flushed face was having trouble getting a six-horse hitch clear of a corral. The animals were edgy, swinging and trampling as the man fought them over to the waiting stage with a steady string of curses. Here, when one of the leaders was slow getting into position, the man, vicious with anger, went after the animal wickedly, beating at its head with the end of a chain tug.

Cornered and desperate, the horse whirled and kicked. One lashing hoof landed with a sodden thud and the man went over backward in a wild, loose fall, arms and legs flailing. He rolled limply once, then lay without move or sound, seeming in some strange way to sink slightly into the trampled earth.

Held to startled stillness for a moment, the miners now crowded around, one of them dropping to a knee beside the crumpled figure. Slowly he regained his feet, blurting with stunned awe.

'Goddlemighty! This here is a dead one. His whole face is smashed in!'

The girl, watching and listening, gave a little cry of distress, and Ellerson, glancing at her, saw her press a hand to her face and turn away. He also saw that the mistreated team was ready to cut and run, and it was entirely natural for him to start quieting them with firm hand and soothing words. The miners gave back from what lay on the ground and the agent came forward, shaking and mumbling.

'Mike Boyle! Ah – the fool – The great fool! So many times I warned him about that damned bottle. And now he lies here dead! Which leaves me without a driver. So there will be *no* stage to Rawhide Creek today.'

Protest was immediate. 'Hell, man – don't say that,' a miner exclaimed. 'There's gold waiting to be dug along that creek and I want to get there. I'll drive your stage.'

'That you will not!' retorted the agent. 'I risk no team and stage at the hands of a miner.'

Recognizing a long chance, Cleve Ellerson now reached quickly for it. 'How about me? I've handled horses all my life and I can handle these. For the price of the ride, I'll take your stage through.'

The agent came about, half angrily. 'You must not hear good. I just said no miner–!'

'That's the whole point of it,' Ellerson cut in. 'I'm not a miner. And I can handle a team and stage as well as any man.'

There was evidence to back up this claim. The team had quieted now, one member of it even rubbing a friendly head against Ellerson's shoulder. Making a careful up and down appraisal and meeting Ellerson's level, steady glance, the agent considered thoughtfully. Finally he nodded.

'I think you might do, at that. It's plain you have a way with horses. Scotty Duncan will likely give me merry hell for trusting a stranger, but on the other hand could give it to me worse if I turn down a reasonable offer to get the stage through. Friend, it's a deal. I get me a driver, you get your ride. There will be a mail sack to take along.'

He hurried off and the jubilant miners began crowding for seats. Beginning to hook up the team, Ellerson had another look at the girl. Denied a place on the stage, and witness to a moment of explosive violence that had left a dead man on the earth, she was a lonely, disconsolate figure, her head lowered, her cheeks pale. Ellerson followed his glance with a guarded murmur.

'That's likely the Rawhide Creek road yonder past that far warehouse. Should you be waiting when I turn the corner, there'll be a place for you on the seat with me. No offense intended, of course.'

Her head lifted, showing him a troubled glance that was grave and searching. She nodded slightly and trudged away.

The agent returned with the mail sack and a pair of stable hands who rolled the dead driver on to a makeshift blanket stretcher and carried him away. Watching, Ellerson shook a regretful head.

'Tough way to die, even though he did ask for it.

Beating a helpless animal over the head with a chain tug –
well–!'

'Just so,' agreed the agent. He then repeated his earlier
words. 'I warned him – plenty of times I warned him. But
he wouldn't leave that bottle alone.' He handed over the
mail sack. 'This is Uncle Sam's business, so guard it well.
Also, keep an eye open for Pony Bob McCart with the
outbound stage. You'll meet him somewhere up around
the summit. And friend – don't make a fool of me!'

Ellerson smiled faintly. 'You can save your worry.' He
tossed the mail sack under the seat and climbed up, reins
in hand. The gambler with the black hat and coat was
there to greet him narrow of face, cold of eye, and with
critical comment.

'I paid for a safe passage in this stage, not a broken neck
at the bottom of some canyon or gulch. I hope you know
your business.'

There was no trace of friendliness in Ellerson's reply.
'You think I don't, you can get the hell off, right here and
now!'

The gambler's glance flickered and slid away. A
bearded miner, holding down space on top, chuckled.

'Well and plainly spoken, brother!'

Ellerson slacked off the brake, the team hit their collars
and the stage rolled. Satisfied that the tall, gaunt-
shouldered man at the reins knew what he was doing, the
agent sighed his relief and turned back to his office.

The girl was waiting where Ellerson had indicated, and
coming even with her he braked to a halt, giving a further
terse order to the man beside him.

'Drop down and give the lady a hand. She's taking your
seat. You'll have to find another place.'

The gambler's narrow face flushed. 'I laid out good
money for this seat and I'm not about to …'

Ellerson cut him short with a biting curtness. 'Don't

argue with me, tinhorn! Get down there and do as you're told or I'll pitch you off on your head!'

Before this opposition the gambler caved, showing a black look before dropping off. He handed up the girl's luggage and steadied her as she scrambled over the wheel. After which, sour and disgruntled, he found comfortless place among the crowded miners who made room for him with muffled, profane protest. Once safely settled, the girl spoke her gravefaced concern.

'I'll feel very guilty should this cause you any trouble.'

'No trouble,' Ellerson assured her. 'None at all.'

Her glance was very clear, very direct. She gave a little shiver of recollection.

'Back there, that was terrible, wasn't it? About the driver dying as he did, I mean. Sometimes life can be so cruel.'

Ellerson tipped a shoulder. 'He got it the way he was handing it out. Me, I could feel for the horse as well as for him.'

Again she studied him with that clear-eyed gravity so much a part of her, seeing a man in his middle thirties. He had good shoulders, though just now a worn denim jumper and calico shirt hung on them with a betraying looseness. The rugged angles of his face were almost too pronounced and an edge of pallor underlay the weather stain of sun and wind in his gaunt cheeks. His deep set eyes were narrowed to a stone-gray, taciturn aloofness which suggested a considerable skepticism of the world and of the men who could make it ugly with their many sordid motives. And though he had shown her a kindness and a courtesy, the manner in which he had handled the gambler suggested an inner explosiveness that could turn him wholly savage when aroused.

Behind them a miner grumbled further protest at the gambler and a flicker of impish amusement replaced the soberness in the girl's glance. 'I supposed I should feel ashamed, robbing that poor man of his seat?'

Ellerson's head shake was decisively abrupt, his words harsh. 'Never be sorry for a tinhorn. They are strictly buzzard breed, always out to pick the bones of some poor devil, or to pull a sneak gun on him!'

Realizing that her remark had stirred up a gust of some kind of smouldering inner feeling, the girl turned silent.

Leaving the flat, the road pitched sharply upward into the timber. Quick to realize he was driving a good and willing team, Ellerson let the horses set their own pace, and they, equally quick to sense a confident hand at the reins, tended strictly to business.

For a time progress was slow, as here the road was badly rutted, and the lurch and jounce of the stage did Ellerson's sore side no good at all. As this misery deepened, his thoughts turned darkly back to the savage moments at the poker table in Border City when he made the mistake of giving a tinhorn the benefit of the doubt and only narrowly survived to regret it.

With the best pot of the evening on the table, the tinhorn, running true to form, went to the bottom of the deck. Caught red handed, he turned so cringing and mealy mouthed, Ellerson's impulse was to merely boot him out of town rather than take the affair more seriously. Therein lay his mistake as the tinhorn, even while whining excuses, was inching a snub-nosed, two shot .41 caliber derringer from a vest pocket.

The gun clear, he reared back and sent a slug smashing into Ellerson's ribs. The impact spun Ellerson from his chair, with the tinhorn making a second try which missed by inches only. Falling, Ellerson got off his single shot, throwing it with the speed and certainty that had made his name a highly respected one during the

Tarpy Grant range trouble. Taken center and heart high, the tinhorn went down on the far side of the table, dead as he hit the floor.

All of which, in the light of what followed, was of little satisfaction then and none at all now, Ellerson reflected soberly. For, as it panned out, while the doctor in Border City had done a first rate professional job on the damaged ribs, he had seen Ellerson as just another tough, drifting rider with a ready gun, and a fee earned was a fee to be collected. Also, weeks of holding down a hotel bed while the bullet wound healed, did not come free. So it was that virtually everything had gone – horse, riding gear, all of it – as it was a strong tenet in Cleve Ellerson's make-up never to leave an unpaid debt of any kind behind him.

The enforced confinement in that run down hotel had been a long and lonely session, from which he emerged nearly flat broke, some twenty pounds lighter than usual, kitten weak and entirely at loose and dubious ends. It had been the lowest, most meager period of existence he had ever known, leaving him deeply thoughtful and with the realization of being at a definite crossroads in life. For he was a riding man completely afoot in a strange town, with no horse, no saddle, no friends, no job and damn little money. So where did the trail lead from here?

Certainly not back to the wild, reckless days of the kind he'd known during the Tarpy Grant trouble, when some men rode for one outfit, some for another, and in the riding and fighting that followed, some of them died. Rough country, rough men, rough days, with nothing permanent or certain, least of all life itself. If a man was to find something worthwhile and enduring in life, then he had to seek out a brand new trail to follow. So he had reasoned and so he had decided when a chance item in a Border City newspaper pointed out that trail for him.

Somewhere over past the Carson Mountains, so the item read, a new, rich placer gold strike had been made on a stream called Rawhide Creek. Golden treasure was coming out of that camp and men were heading there – so why not him?

In consequence he'd spent his last dime for a railroad ticket to Chinese Flat. Now he was sweating out some misery miles up the rutted steepness of this mountain road.

This Carson Mountain country was big and wild, a world of long ridges, deep canyons, and lofted, timbered heights that ran away and away into distant blue silhouette. The season was early spring and in every gulch and canyon, white water tumbled and foamed. For the most part, the miners riding the stage were drifters, following the call of every new gold camp. Over the first few miles from Chinese Flat they had swapped mining talk, spilling tobacco juice and casual profanity with equal carelessness.

Shoulders trimly erect as she balanced to the swing of the stage, the girl beside Ellerson had ridden quietly. But little lines of repressed weariness were beginning to pull her lip corners, and sight of these moved Ellerson to gruff apology.

'Didn't mean to speak you short a while back. We were talking about tinhorns and it happens I've no use for any of the breed. Not too long ago I made the mistake of treating one of them like he was a human being instead of a no good rat, and near got killed for it.'

Again she studied him, appreciating his concern, the more so because he had made no attempt to presume on it. She spoke some quiet concern of her own.

'You've been favouring your side. Also there is a

gauntness that suggests injury or illness of some kind?'

Ellerson's smile was brief and shadowy. 'You have sharp eyes.'

Came further proof of feminine observation and insight. 'When did you eat last?'

The mere suggestion of food tightened Ellerson's jaw and set the juices of raw hunger flooding.

'What makes you ask that?'

'Sharp eyes again, perhaps.'

She leaned and lifted her wicker basket to the seat between them. From it she produced a thick, elk steak sandwich. 'This should help.'

Ellerson looked away, shaking his head. 'Can't rob you of your food.'

'Don't be foolish,' she scolded mildly. 'You're not robbing me. I ate all I wanted back on the train. And you've saved me from having to spend a night in that ratty old hotel at Chinese Flat. So I really do owe you something. You'll find this will taste better than it looks.'

Wolfing it down, Ellerson thought it the best food he'd ever known. Watching with her clear, level glance, the girl nodded.

'Just as I thought. You were famished. Well, there's more of it, Mr ...?'

'Ellerson,' he supplied. 'Cleve Ellerson. You're saving my life, you know. Am I glad I held this seat for you!'

She laughed softly. 'And am I. I'm Holly Yarnell.'

Ellerson waded through another generous sandwich. The food was like a strong jolt of liquor, the way it took hold. It was his turn to study and question her. 'You have friends, or kin at Rawhide Creek?'

'A married sister. How about you? You've not the look of a miner.'

'Never dug an ounce in my life,' he confessed. 'But I may have to. Depends on what I can line up in the way of a job.'

Smiling slightly, she looked straight ahead. 'It is a woman's privilege to be curious. And I am. I'm wondering about your open dislike of gamblers and if some particular experience accounts for it?'

When he did not answer immediately her glance swung around and she was startled at the bleak harshness of his expression. Quickly, she added, 'I'm sorry if I had no right to that question!'

Silent for another short interval, he shrugged. Then he told her his story.

Quick concern widened her eyes. 'You mean – he actually shot you?'

She was so ingenuous about it Ellerson had to show the edge of a grim smile. 'That's what the sawbones decided when he dug the slug out.'

'What – happened to the gambler?'

'He died,' Ellerson said tersely. 'He missed me clean with his second shot – but I didn't miss him.'

'Then he's dead – and you killed him?'

'That's how it worked out.'

She caught her breath sharply, and though still occupying the seat next to him, Ellerson knew the feeling that in some strange way an invisible wall of some sort had suddenly lifted between them, and it moved him to brief qualifying.

'It was him or me.'

Her chin was up, her glances again straight ahead. 'That is the usual excuse, isn't it? Always the other man or you?'

'No excuse,' Ellerson told her dryly. 'Just a fact.'

Now, with most of its miles and the worst stretches left behind, the road swung looping across a wide, gradually climbing benchland toward the final summit. Here the timber thinned and Ellerson began searching ahead for the outbound stage he would be meeting. On the final summit the road ran an almost level way across high, rock-ribbed meadows. Patches of snow still clotted gray granite shoulders and though the sun shone brightly the air was thin and knife keen.

The miners started to liven up, speculating on their chances of hitting it rich on the gravel bars of Rawhide Creek. As he listened, Ellerson knew a dry, sardonic amusement. How many times before had they chased this same elusive, roseate dream, only to find it an empty one?

Beyond the summit the road dipped into thickening timber again, running smoothly through a series of sweeping turns, the traces of the team loose and swinging, the stage rocking easily on its leather thoroughbraces. It was a relaxing moment which Ellerson savored pleasantly. But only for a little time, as just beyond the next turn he was hauling on the reins and riding the brake with such authority the stage lurched wildly before coming to a grinding halt, iron shod wheels squealing protest against tightly locked hickory brake blocks. Just out there ahead another stage and team stood angled across the road, blocking it. By the near front wheel of this outfit a man lay sprawled and still.

Exclaiming with harsh concern, Ellerson looped his reins on the brake handle, jumped to the ground and hurried forward, followed by the bearded miner, Barney Ewalt and several others. The man face down in the road had evidently been riding shotgun guard, as a sawed-off ten gauge Greener double gun lay beside him. He had been shot through the head.

A miner who circled the far side of the stage called further grim words. 'Here's another one. The driver, I think – as he's still tangled with the reins.'

Barney Ewalt picked up the Greener gun, showed Ellerson the unfired shells still in the chambers. 'Poor devil never had a chance. Killed before he could get off a shot. A dirty piece of business.'

Another miner spoke his wonderment. 'The passengers – where would they be?'

'Probably weren't any,' Barney Ewalt said. 'These days people are heading for Rawhide Creek, not away from it. They'll start leaving when the diggin's begin playing out.' He turned to Ellerson again. 'This sort of thing sickens any decent man. What's to do about it?'

'Right now about all we can do is take this stage and these two men back to Rawhide Creek,' Ellerson said. 'Somebody will have to drive. How about you?'

Ewalt shrugged. 'As a kid on a Missouri farm I followed a pair of mules down many a ploughed furrow. If you'll square the outfit for me, I'll give it a try.'

'Good man,' Ellerson approved. 'First I want a look around. While I'm at it, get some help and load these two inside.'

Ellerson tramped back into the timber, eyes on the ground, searching for sign that he knew had to be somewhere. He made three ever widening circles before he found it, a hoof-churned area beyond a dense jackpine thicket, where a pair of restless horses had been tied. Here also lay the treasure box, open and empty, its lock smashed. Further brief search showed the direction by which those horses had come to this spot and how they had left it. Satisfied with these findings, Ellerson shouldered the treasure box and tramped back to the waiting stages.

The luckless driver and the shotgun guard had been laid out carefully on the floor of the empty stage and after loading the treasure box in beside them Ellerson got the stage turned and headed back down grade.

Taking over the reins, Barney Ewalt drove off at an easy pace, accompanied by several miners caught up in a morbid excitement. Jaded and grim, Cleve Ellerson climbed back to the seat of his own rig where a distressed Holly Yarnell sat, white-faced and silent.

TWO

They came upon Rawhide Creek abruptly, the road breaking from the timber into a grassy flatland. Here stretched a long, curving basin, walled on all sides by lofty, timbered hills and slashed through by a brawling stream running amber brown between banks of gravel and ragged thickets of scrub willow and alder. Along the stream men toiled feverishly, some with pick and shovel in shallow pits, some crouched at the edge of the water with swirling gold pans. Still others labored with crude rockers.

At the far end of the basin, just off the mouth of a timber shrouded canyon, the camp itself lay sprawled and unlovely, without pattern or order, men having built anywhere – and anyhow – need or fancy dictated. There were a few fairly substantial larger buildings and a scatter of stout cabins, but in the main whatever offered reasonable shelter against the weather was good enough.

The road skirted the edge of the basin and out ahead Cleve Ellerson saw Barney Ewalt roll the lead stage to a safe halt before one of the larger buildings. Immediately a rush of men gathered and when Ellerson brought his rig in he had to haul up short, blocked by the crowd. A stocky, grizzled man drove sturdy shoulders against the crush, broke through and had his look inside the lead stage, then threw a harsh growl at Barney Ewalt, who answered briefly before nodding in Ellerson's direction. Whereupon the grizzled one hurried over to show Ellerson a hot blue-eyed glance.

'All right – you tell it! I'm Scotty Duncan. I own these stages. Where's my regular whip, Mike Boyle? How's it happen you're driving? How ...?'

'Ease up – ease up!' cut in Ellerson. 'Suppose we see this young lady on her way first. She's anxious to get shut of the whole deal – me included.'

Since their brief exchange of words at the scene of the holdup, Holly Yarnell had been strictly silent. But now she turned on him quickly.

'You didn't have to say that, for I do appreciate the kindness you've shown me. But it isn't always easy to understand some people.'

Scorning any help she scrambled from the stage. Ellerson handed down her luggage, tossed the reins to a hostler who came slouching up, then eased to the ground himself and told Scotty Duncan what had happened.

A man's harsh anger lifted from the crowd. 'Somebody sure owes me something. I had a poke of gold going out on that stage, and now some damn murderin' thief has it. I say what I've said before. This camp needs a miner's court to put ropes around certain necks!'

From another quarter, a broad Irish brogue lifted in warning. 'Best go easy with such talk, Johnny O'Dea – lest it earn you a knife in the back like it did Jim Oliver for speakin' his mind too strong.'

About to move off with her luggage, Holly Yarnell whirled back, eyes wide and dark with sudden shock and fear.

'What's that? What did you say? Jim Oliver – a knife in the back …?'

Startled by the intensity of the girl's reaction, the speaker answered bluntly. "Tis common word along the creek, Miss. Happened a week ago.'

'But you don't understand!' she wailed. 'Jim Oliver is my sister's husband. You can't mean that he – that he is – is…?' She couldn't bring out the dread word.

Instantly the miner was wholly kind, reassuring her. 'Oh, no – Jim's not dead, or likely to be. But he's a sore shoulder to nurse.'

As the girl hurried off, a late arrival pushed through the crowd. A tall, dark-faced man with a sheriff's badge on his shirt. He spoke with curt authority.

'What's the trouble here, Duncan? What's this talk about a holdup and some dead men?'

Rumbling a deep anger, Scotty Duncan faced the newcomer. 'All true enough, Jack Pelly. A treasure box looted and two good men shot down. Pony Bob McCart and Jake Rivers. Take a look and see if they're dead enough to suit you!'

The dark-faced one peered into the stage, then came around, swart features flushed. 'I don't like what you said or the way you said it, Duncan. Maybe you better explain.'

Scotty Duncan gave back not a doughty inch. 'I've thought it and said it before, Pelly. This camp needs law and order for others besides Duke Ackerman. You carry the badge, so you're the man to see to that. Here is murder and robbery, tossed right in your lap. What are you going to do about it?'

'Do? Do what I can, of course.' Jack Pelly's dark cheeks showed deepening resentment. 'Hell, man! I don't like this sort of thing any more than you. But I can't stop a stage holdup taking place miles from where I happen to be, and I can't bring dead men back to life.'

'I'd never ask the impossible of any man,' persisted Scotty, stubbornly dogged, 'but I do expect a real effort here and I'll have plenty to say around this camp if I don't get it.' A turn of his head indicated Ellerson. 'This man can tell you where the holdup took place. Starting from there you should be able to come up with something.'

Jack Pelly's quick glance measured Ellerson. 'Haven't seen you before, so you must be new here. And I like to know all the boys.'

Ellerson named himself. 'You'll see where the outbound stage was turned on a switchback a little way this side of the summit.'

Pelly nodded. 'I'll have a look. But this is big, wild country, and running down a trail in it is no easy chore.'

He went quickly away. Scotty Duncan stared after him, growling harsh doubt. 'Take a look, maybe – but probably all you'll do.'

With its initial morbid curiosity satisfied, the crowd began to scatter and drift uptown and Cleve Ellerson, having fulfilled his obligation to the stage line, followed along, his thoughts somber.

This camp of Rawhide Creek gained nothing on closer inspection. It was crude and unlovely in every way. As was the deadfall Ellerson approached. A building long and low of roof, built in part of logs and part of raw, rough sawn lumber. A crude sign above its open door proclaimed the place THE LUCKY LODE. That same door let out a rumble of sound. The tramp and scoff of heavy, restless boots. The loud talk of men still reasonably sober and an occasional raucous shout by some who were not. About to enter the place, Ellerson listened to the growl of threatening words.

'... for the last time, Kenna – I'm tellin' you to get out of here, and stay out! You're just a no good, lousy, drink

cadging bum and the boss don't want you hangin'
around bothering the trade. Maybe this will make you
understand I mean business …!'

There sounded the impact of a blow and a man reeled
from the door, near to falling as he collided with
Ellerson, who instinctively caught and steadied him.
Under the ragged clothes the man was thin and wasted,
with a face seamed and ravaged by years of too much
whiskey. The one who had hit him and now stood in the
deadfall doorway was a barroom bouncer, burly and
scowling.

Secure on his feet again, and mopping dazedly at a
spreading smear of crimson on his bruised mouth and
chin, the clubbed one stumbled off, mumbling his
bruised and seething feelings. The bouncer called
Morley spat into the street before putting a challenging
stare on Ellerson.

'If you're a friend of his, you better move on, too!'

It was on Ellerson's tongue to tell the fellow off in
kind, but he checked the impulse.

'Never saw him before.'

The bouncer spat again and turned back. Ellerson
followed inside and found a place against the wall from
which to have his look over the room. Then a
restraining hand closed on his arm and he looked down
at the owner of it. Here was a lean, Indian-brown man
with eyes and hair as black as those of any Indian. The
black-eyed glance was steady, the hand on his arm
sinewy.

'Name's Jeffers,' said the man. 'Sash Jeffers. Scotty
Duncan sent me. He wants a talk with you.'

'Why with me?' Ellerson demanded. 'What would he
want to talk about with me?'

Sash Jeffers shrugged. 'You brought the stages in,
didn't you? Well, no squarer man than Scotty Duncan

ever lived. Mebbe he figgers he owes you somethin', and what Scotty Duncan owes, he pays.'

They started for the door but a surge of men drove them back. Just inside the street door a miner stood, his leathery face full of anger and contorted with dark purpose. He sent a harsh challenge down the room.

'All right, Ackerman, show yourself. Come on out of your back room kennel. You hear me – come on out – or I move in after you!'

Nobody came from the back room to answer the miner's call. But the black clad faro lookout came off his stool with catlike swiftness. He was dapper and trim and moved with a controlled confidence that made him deadly.

'You've come far enough, Tomlin – and said a big plenty. You saw and talked with Mr. Ackerman yesterday, and where he is concerned, your business with him was settled then.'

'Different here, Rindler!' was the heated return. 'My business with Duke Ackerman won't be settled until he gets his sluice boxes off my claim. This time I'm calling that damned thief cold! And I'm going into that back room after him!'

The miner moved forward and the man in black rocked up on his toes. 'For the last time, Tomlin – far enough!'

So wild was the miner's state of mind the warning meant nothing to him. He cursed and clawed a rusty old bulldog revolver from a coat pocket. The purpose was direct enough but the effort far too slow and awkward. He had his ancient weapon only half clear when the man in black whipped a gun from a shoulder holster and shot him dead in his tracks. Even as the miner crumpled down, the man in black shot him a second time. It was fast, deadly and wicked.

Taut silence followed the hard, pounding echoes of the shots. And now, finally, the rear door did open and a fleshy, florid-faced man stood there, sharply calling.

'What is this, Al – what is this?'

The man in black braced his shoulders against the bar, his pale eyes roving the room warily, judging its reaction. His reply was thin and exact.

'Tomlin again, Duke. Except that this time he was really off the reservation. He was out to gun you. Me, too! I tried to warn him off, but he wouldn't listen. So-o-o!' Al Rindler shrugged his lithe shoulders.

Came another voice, the same one Ellerson had heard earlier when he brought the stages in. 'Ned Tomlin was a good man, and honest, Al Rindler. It wasn't necessary that you kill him!'

Al Rindler came up on his toes again, staring toward the speaker, amber eyes glinting and hard. 'I did only what I had to do. It was him or me. He went for his gun first. And any man who sets out to throw a gun on me, has got to finish the ride. And as usual, of course, you *would* have something to say, eh O'Dea? I've heard it said that every once in a while your kind talk themselves into an early grave.'

'But not today, Rindler,' was the steady reply. 'I've no gun on me to give you the usual excuse. And at night, not trusting you or your kind at all in the dark, I'll be watchful. Now, who's to help me carry out this poor lad?'

There was a short moment of hesitation before three silent, sober faced men stepped forward. Al Rindler, the dapper killer, watched coolly until they were gone with their limp, sagging burden, then turned to join the florid faced man and retreat with him into the back room.

Silent and impassive, Cleve Ellerson observed and

heard it all. It was something he had seen before – men cut down by slashing lead, and he was thinking that the surroundings made little account when violent death marched. He turned to Sash Jeffers.

'Well, we saw it. Now we can get out of here.'

'That Al Rindler,' murmured Jeffers carefully. 'He's a wolf – a dirty, killing wolf. Ned Tomlin – that miner – he didn't stand even a thin chance.'

'That's right,' Ellerson agreed. 'He didn't.'

Outside, the day was near done and the darkening street fairly empty. With twilight closing in the air was increasingly bitter. Fat pine fires spread pungent layers of resin-scented smoke across the thickening dusk and from somewhere close at hand came the good fragrance of frying meat to taunt and deepen a man's hunger. Down street a big freight outfit lumbered into town. Sash Jeffers pointed.

'One of Scotty's. He started with a single team and spring wagon. Now he owns that Merivale double-hitch outfit and two more like it, along with his stage business. He's a doer, Scotty is.'

Hurrying at Ellerson's side, Sash Jeffers guided him to a building tucked close to the dark loom of a warehouse where the newly arrived freight outfit had pulled to a halt. Further back were corrals and feed sheds and a long, narrow building combining both a bunkhouse and cook shack. From this now a hostler came hurrying to take over the freighter's string of weary mules.

The room Sash Jeffers led Cleve Ellerson into was a sizeable one, and except for the strict necessities, spartan plain. One corner held a desk and a couple of chairs. In another were shelves of grub supplies and kitchen utensils. Creaking with heat, a sheepherder stove filled the room's center along with a table and some more chairs. Blanketed bunks stood along two opposite walls. At the foot of one of these bulked an oak strong box, reinforced with massive iron straps and secured with a hasp and lock equally massive.

There was a rear door and window. Beside the door a bench held water pails and a tin wash basin and some towels hung from a nail in the door post. Scattered wall pegs held odds and ends of clothing. There was a rack with a pair of Winchester rifles, a sawed off shotgun, a cartridge belt with a holstered sixgun, and beside it a shelf holding several boxes of ammunition. The desk was stacked with waybills and invoices and, behind it, in the down-pouring light of a hanging lamp, Scotty Duncan sat.

Curious about this man, Cleve Ellerson now took closer account of him than before. Under a thatch of grizzled hair was a face of blunt, pugnacious features, with bristling brows and frosty blue eyes that seemed to fairly blaze, so intense was the spirit behind them. First words were a gruff rumble.

'Where'd you find him, Sash?'

'In the Lucky Lode,' Jeffers said. 'Saw something else there, too. Al Rindler gunned down a miner named Ned Tomlin, who was trying to get at Duke Ackerman. It was mean, Scotty – close to being outright murder.'

Scotty Duncan came up straighter in his chair. 'What was the excuse, this time?'

Sash Jeffers related the incident briefly, and Scotty shook his head with deep, angry regret. 'That damned hell-hole!'

Stepping from the chill outer world into the warmth of this one brought about a reaction that sent a shiver through Cleve Ellerson and made him pull his gaunt shoulders together. Not missing this, Scotty Duncan spoke again quickly, and with milder tone.

'Man – Man – get next to that stove. Sash, mix him a toddy!'

Sash Jeffers brought a bottle and glass. He poured a good three fingers of whiskey and added water from the kettle steaming on the stove. Cradling the glass in both hands, Ellerson backed up to the stove and sipped the hot drink with a keen relish, conscious of Scotty's intense, measuring scrutiny.

'First,' Scotty rumbled, 'I'd thank you for bringing my stages through. Also the two men who died in that holdup. Good and faithful men, both of them and a loss I can ill afford. I grieve over them, and given the opportunity, I hope to wipe out the scum who killed them. But now, if you don't mind, I'd ask you a question or two. Mind telling me what brought you to this camp?'

Ellerson shrugged. 'Empty pockets that are still empty. I've got to line up a job of some sort, if I'm to eat and have a bunk to sleep in.'

'Just so,' nodded Scotty. 'That is what I want to talk about.' He looked at Jeffers. 'Go get your supper, Sash. Tell the cook not to hold anything over for me. I'll probably eat at Jim Oliver's place.'

As Sash Jeffers left, Scotty returned his glance to Ellerson. 'I will speak plainly, right from the first, so that there will be no misunderstanding. I have need of a man, a very special kind of man. One who can handle other men, amicably if possible, ruthlessly if that be necessary. A man of judgment who can accept responsibility and face up to very probable danger. And above all, a man I can trust implicitly. A large order, true enough, but such a man will be well paid, very well indeed! Are you interested?'

Cleve Ellerson met and held Scotty's boring glance while he gave grave answer. 'Sure I'm interested. It sounds like a job, and that's what I'm looking for. As you say, you've laid out a large order, one which makes me wonder some. Now why should you trust me, when you know so little about me?'

'Because,' growled Scotty, 'the way things are shaping up for me, I've got to trust somebody. And I've the feeling I can trust you because you brought my stages through.'

Savoring the welcome tide of warmth it sent through him, Ellerson drained his glass, his thoughts racing over the requirements Scotty Duncan had catalogued. Could he really fulfill them? And while this grizzled man with the steely blue eyes appeared willing to place full trust in him, could he give the same trust in return? Of two things, however, he could be sure. Here was challenge, but here also was opportunity. So decision came and Ellerson voiced it soberly.

'You've shown me your cards and have the right to a look at mine. I am not running away from anything. I can't claim the accumulation of much except considerable experience in the ways of my fellow man. There is nothing along my back trail to be overly ashamed of, and I have, with fair success, bossed other men on occasion. Also, along the trail I've met with enough danger of one sort or another, not to worry at the prospect of more of it. Past that I'm just as you see me, and if you're still willing to gamble on me, then I'm your man.'

Scotty Duncan was quickly up and around the desk with outstretched hand. 'We'll shake on that! But first, there is one more thing before we go get supper.' At Ellerson's wondering glance he smiled grimly. 'Over here,' he said, moving to the room's rear wall. 'Take a look at this.' He fingered a bullet hole in the wall.

'Happened night before last,' Scotty went on. 'I had to run over to the warehouse for a minute or two, so left the light burning. Somebody was waiting to catch me against the light when I returned and opened the door Tried to shoot me in the back. I was lucky. They pulled a trifle wide. The slug gouged some splinters from the door post and dug into this wall here. Gives you an idea about the possible danger I mentioned. Does it make you consider changing your mind?'

Ellerson's headshake was emphatically negative. 'Just smartens me up and makes me glad I still have this.'

He opened the flap of his jumper to show the butt of the big Colt gun tucked in the waistband of his jeans. 'I know what gunsmoke is. I've smelled my share of it.'

Scotty exclaimed softly. 'You wouldn't be carrying that if you didn't know how to use it?'

'If I didn't know, I wouldn't be here now.' Ellerson's reply was grimly dry.

Scotty growled his satisfaction. 'I'm liking our deal better all the time.'

THREE

The eating house was only a little way along the street from Scotty's quarters, its light a dim yellow blur beyond steam misted windows.

'Jim Oliver's place,' Scotty explained. 'Him and his Missus own it. Right now Jim's laid up. On his way home from a miner's meeting about a week ago somebody tried to stick a knife in his back. Out to kill him, I guess, but ended up just cuttin' him some. Feller run before Jim could tell who it was. Now Mrs. Oliver is nigh workin' herself to death, keepin' things going until Jim can help again. Dirty damned shame! Makes a man boil, some of the things happenin' in this camp.'

They stood aside for some miners to leave, then went in and sat up to a roughly built, but clean-scrubbed counter. Warm food odors swirled, mocking a hunger in Cleve Ellerson so raw and demanding he sat with sagging head until movement and brief words beyond the counter straightened him up.

'It will have to be venison stew, as that is all we have left.'

Facing him and Scotty was Holly Yarnell, trim and neat in blue and white checked gingham. The rich luxury of her hair was tied back from cheeks flushed with kitchen heat. Her clear-eyed glance was cool and impersonal. Ellerson exclaimed.

'So you're about to feed me again?'

'If the stew will suit.'

'Anything!' Ellerson told her fervently. 'Just so there is plenty of it.'

Scotty added his rumbling remark. 'Sure pleasures me to see you here, lass. Someone to help Mrs. Oliver. Since Jim's trouble she's been a driven slave to the hunger of mankind.'

'I'm happy to be here,' the girl replied simply. 'We'll make out, Helen and me.'

She brought them stew, hot biscuits and coffee. 'That,' she announced, 'will be a dollar apiece.'

Scotty laid out the money and she hurried off, gathering up an armful of dishes the miners had used. To keep from wolfing his food, Ellerson forced himself to look around. The kitchen proper was separated from the serving counter by a short, half high wall. Beyond this he saw the girl say something to an older, graying, care-worn woman laboring with pots and pans on a cluttered stove top. Later, the woman came around to pour more coffee and show Ellerson a direct glance.

'I'm Helen Oliver,' she said. 'And knowing the concern of an older sister, I'm thanking you for seeing Holly through from Chinese Flat.'

'Glad I was of use,' Ellerson said. 'Though it wasn't much. Just a matter of finding room for her on the stage.'

'It was more than that,' Helen Oliver insisted. 'It was safety for her. This is rough and wild country with more than its rightful share of the vicious and the scoundrelly. Sometimes I think there is no safety for decent folk here at all. And certainly there is no law.'

Ellerson nodded sympathetically. 'Isn't there suppose to be, Ma'am? I saw a man wearing a star. Fellow named Pelly.'

Helen Oliver sniffed scornfully, a flash of indignant spirit in her tired eyes. 'Jack Pelly's law is entirely Duke Ackerman's law, which is no law at all for anybody else!'

She retreated to her kitchen and two hungry men finished their meal to the last biscuit crumb and drop of coffee.

Back in quarters again, the hanging lamp once more aglow, Ellerson immediately sought a place by the stove. Scotty surveyed him with narrowed eyes.

'You've no coat – no other clothes?'

Smiling ruefully, Ellerson ran a hand along a worn, faded and threadbare jumper sleeve. 'You're looking at all there are. And they've been with me a considerable time.'

Scotty grunted, brought a leather pouch from a coat pocket and spilled a clutter of gold coins on a corner of his desk. 'Take this, get you over to the trading post and buy yourself a new outfit. You'll find the place open, as Pete Yost is a shrewd, money-making little devil who believes in using up all of every day. His layout is right across from the eating house.'

Peter Yost was short, rotund and definitely shrewd of eye. At Ellerson's order he laid out razor and soap, new clothes inside and out, a canvas, blanket-lined coat and a caddy of Durham tobacco. Ellerson gathered up his bundles, pocketed his change and hurried out.

During his absence, Ellerson found that Scotty had put a couple of buckets of water on the stove to heat. 'Knew you'd want to clean up. The water's hot. And you'll be bunking in here with me.'

A decent interval later, buoyed by a feeling of physical well-being he had not known since before the dreary days in Border City, Ellerson pulled up a chair and faced Scotty across the desk.

'All right, Scotty – you've made it possible for me to

feel like a regular human being again. You've opened
the book a little way. How's for a look at the rest of it so
I'll know exactly what you're paying me for?'

Scotty pushed aside the stack of freight invoices he'd
been checking. A glint of grim satisfaction flickered in
his frosty blue eyes.

'I was wondering when you'd get around to asking
that. I started a one-man business with a team of horses
and a spring wagon. It ran away with me, for now I've
three double-hitch Merivale freight outfits steadily on
the road and I could use a fourth. Also, I've a stage line
to keep in some kind of operation. My immediate affairs
reach from here to Chinese Flat, and could spread
further at any time. I've a crew of men to handle and
keep in line. Human contrariness being what it is, there
are always problems stirring there. Most of my crew are
good men. Two of the best were those I lost in that
holdup yesterday.'

Scotty paused, staring soberly off into nothing.
Presently he resumed. 'Of the one I lost at Chinese Flat,
I must say this. I regret Mike Boyle's death and the
manner of it, but I was about to get rid of him because
he was no longer reliable. The men in my bunkhouse
need to be bossed by a fair and steady hand. So I need
help up at the top. A foreman, a manager – call it what
you will. So I have hired you.'

Ellerson broke out a fresh sack of Durham, spun up a
cigarette, nursed the sputtering flame of a sulphur
match in cupped palms. 'I still wonder at your picking
me, a stranger, over someone you've known longer and
better.'

'I've tried others,' Scotty admitted. 'But men with the
proper makeup for the job are not easily come by. Don't
ask me to explain why I feel you are such a man – but I
do. Perhaps I see in you a quality and strength I have

not seen in others. I have tried Buck Devlin, but he will not do. His way with other men is wrong. Too temperish, too unreasonable, too rough and heavy tongued. You cannot curse and abuse men and expect the best from them in return. There is a time to be firm and a time to be flexible. And always a time to lead. Devlin cannot seem to understand this, so you are replacing him.'

Past narrowed eyes, Ellerson mused his wry observation. 'Could be the making of an argument there. From your description, he won't take easy losing out to a stranger. While we're on the subject there is something to be made clear. When I boss men, Scotty, I handle them the way I figure I have to. I can and will meet any man half way, even more than half way. But if nothing else will do, then I can be tough as the next. And when I have to be, I don't want to be second-guessed, even by you, Scotty.'

'I would never interfere against proper authority,' Scotty assured. 'But we must consider something I spoke of earlier. The prospect of danger for you. The word will soon get around that you are my man. Therefore in some places you will not be popular.'

'Such as?'

'Duke Ackerman's deadfall, the Lucky Lode, principally. For us, that is renegade country, thief country. Ackerman hates me, because I know him for what he is and have so stated to his face as well as on other occasions when I felt honest men were listening.

'Then there is more – and worse. Ackerman already has his men working on two claims that he jumped, and he'll steal more if he can. Ned Tomlin, the man you saw Al Rindler shoot down, was the rightful owner of one of those claims. And Danny Yokum, who was a partner of Jim Oliver through a grubstake deal, owned the other claim, and has said so at several miners' meetings. He was on his way home from such a meeting when he was knifed in the back.

'Since I've spoken my mind in similar fashion there has been the shot that put a bullet hole in yonder wall. So there you have it. Does it scare you?'

Ellerson stepped over to the stove and dumped his cigarette butt there. When he turned back there was something cold and formidable about him.

'Not too much,' he said evenly. 'I've met with a few of the Duke Ackermans of this world and have learned a thing or two about them. And now, if you don't mind, I'll hit that bunk you say is waiting for me.'

Scotty nodded. 'Help yourself. Take the one by the window.'

Gray morning light and gray morning chill filled the room when Ellerson awoke. Across the room, Scotty Duncan snored resonantly. Enormously rested and conscious of a strong tide of resurgent physical wellbeing, Ellerson pushed aside his blankets and dressed hurriedly against the chill. He built a fire, then washed in water so icy it stung his cheeks and quickened his breath. After which he crowded the stove, waiting for the coffee to turn over.

The coffee began to steam, giving off its hot fragrance, which brought Scotty out of his blankets and speeded his dressing.

'We'll have a cup of that, then take breakfast with the crew. Give you a chance to look them over.'

The cluttered length of Scotty's bunkhouse furnished quarters for a full dozen men. A second room held a long center table where the crew ate. Beyond and adjoining this was the cook's country. Breakfast was on the table when Scotty and Ellerson went in, and Scotty's rumble of greeting ended in a brief and pointed statement.

'Meet Cleve Elllerson, men. Your new foreman. He has my full confidence. You will take orders from him as you would from me.'

Every eye settled on Ellerson as he found place at the table. It was a measuring, a gauging like he'd met before in outfits he'd ramrodded during the wild days of the Tarpy Grant range war, and it did not greatly concern him on meeting with it again.

From across the table, Sash Jeffers broke the ice with a faint grin. 'You look considerable better than yesterday. Not so frazzled out.'

Ellerson chuckled. 'A square meal and a full night's sleep sure ties a man together.'

The cook was a stumpy, whiskery little individual who moved with a limp and wore a flour sack for an apron. His eyes shone terrier bright as he laid a heaping breakfast plate before Ellerson. 'Me,' he announced, 'I'm Ozzie Sipe, the best cook this side the Rockies. You eat steady with me, friend – you'll soon fill out your clothes.'

Ellerson chuckled again. 'That must be so. Never saw a crew of men looking better fed than this one.'

Ozzie Sipe gave a little hopping shuffle of pleasure. 'Now that's a fact. Eat hearty. More where this comes from. Scotty knows how to keep a cook happy. Gives me free rein.'

A corral hand who had been at some early chores, spoke. 'Don't throw out any scraps, Ozzie. Saw that old bum, Lafe Kenna, out by a feed shed little bit ago. He sure had the shakes. He'll be around for his usual handout.'

The cook eyed Scotty Duncan cautiously. 'I never waste anything fit for a human. And I'm sorry for old

Lafe – he can' help bein' what he is. He gets nothin' but left-overs.'

Past a grim smile, Scotty spoke gruffly. 'I doubt a cup of coffee and a plate of bacon and flapjacks now and then will hurt the commissary.'

'Knew it!' exulted Ozzie Sipe as he skipped back to his stove. 'Knew the boss wouldn't mind.'

Attitudes eased and talk rumbled along the table. As he ate, Cleve Ellerson dropped his glance here and there, touching each man while making quick estimate. Pretty much his own kind, these were. Men of the open, weathered and brown from sun and wind. Teamsters, wagon men, corral hands, with the dust of the open road's far miles and the taint of horse and mule sweat on them. One brown faced, brawny fellow with enormous shoulders and arms like oak logs, had blacksmith written all over him and showed a friendly grin when he caught Ellerson's eye. Different however was the reaction from the far end of the table. There a lank, roan-headed one showed a glance distinctly hostile.

These men all had a day of work ahead of them, so there was no dawdling over their food. They were soon finished, up and about. Scotty had word for one of his teamsters.

'I'll be making the trip over the summit to Chinese Flat with you today, Rory.'

Back in the office, Scotty stuffed various items into a battered leather satchel while explaining to Ellerson. 'I'll be away for a couple of days, Cleve. It's been too long since I was last at Chinese Flat, and needful that I take care of a number of things there. While I'm gone you can get the feel of things here. You can count on most of the men doing their jobs on schedule. Sash Jeffers runs the warehouse and he's a good one. You any ideas about yourself?'

'A couple, maybe,' Ellerson nodded. 'When you get back I'm saddling a horse and taking a ride. Two men pulled that holdup on you, Scotty. I found where they had tied their horses. Coming and going, they had to leave trail sign, and I want to run it down and see where it leads. What say?'

Between narrowed lids, Scotty Duncan's blue eyes glinted. 'Good man! You've a head on you. But never forget that bullet hole in yonder wall and what put it there.'

Outside, the day was a fine one, the whole run of the flats sparkling in the bright pour of the sun. Even the careless sprawl of the camp seemed less offensive to the eyes. Due no doubt, Ellerson decided wryly, to an attitude refreshed and renewed by food, rest, and a rewarding upturn in his personal fortunes, rather than by any real improvement in the face of the camp. In any event it was fine to know this renewed vigor with which to meet a vigorous world.

Activity along the flats was the same as yesterday, men toiling in their various ways to get at the yellow treasure that gave point to their efforts. For the most part they paid Ellerson little attention as he sauntered along, being too engrossed in their own affairs to pay heed to a casual passerby. In one place only did he meet with any show of suspicion or hostility. He had circled the far lower end of the flats and was on his way back to town when he came even with a couple of dripping sluice boxes. Men swung busy shovels, slopping earth and gravel into a strong head of muddy water. One of the shovelers looked Ellerson over with a surly belligerence and growled harsh rebuff.

'Move along! No business here for you. Move along!'

Quelling a stir of anger, Ellerson shrugged and passed on. He wanted no quarrel here, but the bite of anger held and made him wonder. Out ahead a miner crouched at the creek edge, swirling a gold pan. He grinned tiredly up at Ellerson.

'Tough way to make a living, brother.'

Ellerson got out his tobacco and spun up a smoke. 'Never tried it myself, but I can see what you mean.' He jerked his head toward the sluice boxes. 'That looks like an easier way.'

The miner grunted. 'If you got the money to build 'em and hire help. I ain't – but Duke Ackerman has. That was Danny Yokum's Discovery claim. But it's Ackerman's now and he's gettin' rich off it and a couple more he's snagged on to. But most fellers like me, we scratch out bacon and beans and once in a while a bottle of whiskey. Mainly we live on hope. Maybe the next pan will be a fat one. Well, like I say – here's hopin'!'

Reaching town, Ellerson headed for the Lucky Lode, the place Scotty Duncan had designated a hell-hole. Last night Helen Oliver used milder words but inferred the same. And yesterday afternoon he himself had seen a man shot to death in the dive under unsavory circumstance. So now he wanted another look at the place with a more searching and discerning eye.

Where the sun struck strongly at the base of a wall, a man hunkered, shrunken and disheveled. The face he showed Ellerson was lined and whiskey ravaged. Stirring, he spoke huskily.

'Ain't you the one who kept me on my feet yesterday after Tug Morley slugged me? Didn't thank you then, so I do now.'

'You'd maybe be Kenna?' Ellerson asked. 'Lafe Kenna?'

'The same. Lafe Kenna. A bum who's no good to himself or to the rest of the world. And right now,' he added, his voice thinning to a taut whisper, 'near dyin' for need of a drink!'

'Well, now,' Ellerson said quickly, 'I was just going in for a drink, myself. You come along and have one with me.'

He took Kenna by the arm, felt the shaking torment in the man as he led him inside. Things were slack in the deadfall at this time of day. Only a thin scatter of patrons were at the bar and the lone poker game in progress was a four-handed affair, one of the players being the gambler who had come in on the stage with Ellerson from Chinese Flat. Another one was Jack Pelly, the sheriff. The faro layout was idle, the lookout stool empty. And the man who usually occupied it, Al Rindler, the tawny, cat-like one, was watching the poker game. Tug Morley was bellied against the bar, toying with a glass of whiskey.

'No you don't,' he blustered. 'I told you that you were all through cadging drinks in here, Kenna. Mr. Ackerman wants no dirty, lousy bum bothering the trade.'

Impulse had swayed Cleve Ellerson when he invited Lafe Kenna in with him. Now it was a quick, hot anger that took hold.

'What are you so proud about, Morley? You're a hell of a way from being any prize specimen, yourself. Right now you're the one bothering the trade. I'm buying a drink and Lafe is having one with me. Step aside!'

Morley's answer was to throw a heavy shoulder against Kenna, shoving him back. The next moment it was Morley who was rocking on his heels, gulping for air, as Ellerson drove a savage elbow into the fellow's flacid middle. He followed this up with equally savage words.

'I've had a big plenty of you. Get the hell out of my way while you're able to!'

Spread hands pressed against his punished paunch, Morley backed off, reaching hungrily for air. And then it was Al Rindler, stealthy and purring, who took his place.

'What is this? Trouble here? Mister, would you be bringing me trouble?'

A high, gaunt figure, Ellerson eyed him harshly. 'Any time I bring you trouble you won't have to ask about it – you'll know it's arrived. Now I'm about to buy drinks for myself and my friend, Lafe Kenna. Your pal Morley wasn't listening good. How about you?'

For a little time, Rindler gave no answer, his pale eyes moiling. Then the tawny glance filmed and slid away.

'Part of our business is to sell liquor, of course. So long as it's paid for, it will be all right, this time.'

'This, or any other time!' While at it, Ellerson made it positive.

The bartender, uneasily watching and listening, waited for Al Rindler's nod before setting out bottle and glasses. Ellerson poured a short one for himself and a hefty one for Lafe Kenna. To keep from slopping his liquor when he lifted it, the old fellow had to cradle the glass in both hands. But once he had the drink safely put away he steadied. Carefully he returned the glass to the bar and when the bartender moved off to serve an impatient miner further along, he looked up at Ellerson, mumbling his thanks and further guarded words.

'Friend, you'll never know how I needed that drink. Hope it don't cause you trouble with Al Rindler, because he's a bad one, a real bad one.'

Ellerson dropped a brief laugh. 'Let me worry about that. And you can't walk on one leg.' He poured Kenna a second drink, watched him put it away, tossed a coin on the bar and moved back out to the street. Here Lafe Kenna paused, hesitant.

'Can't figger why you set up those drinks for me. You don't owe me nothin' – not an old souse like me. Why'd you do it?'

Ellerson looked along the street, smiling faintly. 'Right off the griddle, I'm not entirely sure. Maybe I'm a born rebel, with a streak of the maverick in me, and not liking to see people pushed around. Maybe I wanted to sound out a few reactions by tossing a rock in the pool and seeing how far the ripples reached.'

'Well now I wouldn't know nothin' about that,' Kenna mumbled. 'But you watch yourself. Al Rindler ain't never goin' to forget somebody who made him take water!'

Leaving old Lafe to again seek comfort in a sun that had climbed to midday, Ellerson headed back to the compound, pulled along by the bite of hunger.

FOUR

Back in the Lucky Lode, Tug Morley leaned against the bar and cursed his blustering distress to Al Rindler. 'Now just who in hell is that one? He was around yesterday for a time. Why would he be nursin' a worthless old dog like Lafe Kenna? All the earmarks of a trouble hunter, you ask me.' Morley pressed his hands against his punished midriff. 'Like to caved a rib on me.'

The poker game had broken up and now Jack Pelly came over. Rindler turned to him. 'That one just in here with Lafe Kenna – maybe you know something about him? Ever see him before?'

'Yesterday,' Pelly nodded. 'Brought in the stage. When I sounded him out he gave his name as Ellerson.'

'What do you make of him?'

'Only one thing for certain. He's no miner.'

'Had a real big chip on his shoulder,' Rindler said. 'I wonder why?'

Pelly shrugged. 'Your guess is as good as mine.'

Rindler's lids drew down in a troubled frown. 'Always a reason for a chip. We better see what Duke thinks.'

They pushed into the back room where Duke Ackerman filled a chair behind a table holding a bottle and glass. He was a big, untidy man with florid jowls and the look of having gone soft from too much food and drink and soft living. His coat was overly tight across his shoulders and neither it or the rumpled, once white shirt under it met completely across the swell of his belly. But though his body looked soft, his eyes did not. Slightly protuberant, they were murky brown, shiny and hard as bottle glass. A contentious, greedy petulance pulled his lips into a thin, down-curving line. Some of that petulance flared now.

'Damn it, Al – how many times do I have to tell you I don't want you fellows busting in here without knocking?'

'Take it easy!' retorted Rindler curtly. 'Nobody is coming through that door who shouldn't. I'll see to that. But there's a stranger in camp I think you should know about. Not a miner. He drove the stage in from Chinese Flat yesterday. Name's Ellerson. That mean anything to you?'

'What makes you think it would?' demanded Ackerman, still cranky.

A faint flush touched Rindler's pale cheeks and his tone took on an edge. 'Duke – I said, go easy! I'm only asking.'

'Never heard the name before,' admitted Ackerman, turning mild. 'What about him?'

Rindler related the barroom incident briefly. 'He sure had a chip on his shoulder. The why of that I can't figure.'

Ackerman pondered, his protuberant eyes clouding. 'Somebody imported by Duncan, do you think?'

Jack Pelly spoke up. 'According to Deuce Carmody, your new house gambler, Duncan's regular whip came off second best with a horse at Chinese Flat, and this Ellerson drove the stage through for the price of the ride. Carmody rates him a tough one.'

Ackerman scowled. 'If he can drive a stage, Duncan can use him.' He thought about this for a moment before switching his glance to Tug Morley. 'At times,

Tug – you act like you had no more brains than a pig. If this Ellerson wanted to bring Lafe Kenna in for a drink, what of it?'

'But you said you didn't want Kenna hangin' around, botherin' the trade,' blurted Morely defensively.

'That's right, I did – and I don't. What I meant was I didn't want him underfoot along the bar, cadging drinks. But if somebody wants to bring him in like this Ellerson did, that's different. Now get on back out there and start acting smart for a change.'

Morley shuffled out. About to follow, Pelly stopped and turned at Ackerman's call. 'A minute, Jack!'

Ackerman looked up at him as Pelly came back. 'You're the one most out and around. What's the talk in camp and how's the feeling?'

'Plenty of both.' Pelly was blunt about it. 'How close to the blow up point though, I couldn't say. But it's there – make no mistake about that. Scotty Duncan's plain about how he feels. He keeps saying openly that we're a flock of damned thieves.' A sardonic twist touched Pelly's lips as he added, 'Smart man, Scotty – damn smart man! And though Jim Oliver isn't up and around too much, he primes them with plenty of tough talk. Then there's that miner, Johnny O'Dea. A real firebrand, that fellow – the sort other miners will listen to and follow. Finally, coming right on top of the stage haul, the Ned Tomlin killing isn't doing us a lick of good.'

Al Rindler flared. 'What the hell! Tomlin had a gun and was on the shoot. I had to stop him.'

To this Ackerman agreed quickly. 'Al did what he had to do. Tomlin brought it on himself. He was a fool.'

'Just so, seeing that he's dead,' remarked Pelly dryly. 'But it is still the sort of thing that could hang us all. It might be smart to go easy for a while. Give the camp a chance to quiet down.'

Ackerman scrubbed an irritable hand across his face. 'Question is, can we afford to, with the kind of setup we got here? A camp like this can boom over night, and go to hell just about as fast. Who knows when these diggings will play out? Not you, not me – not anybody. So we make it while things are good, even though we have to press our luck and take some chances. And in the doing we get rid of whoever is in our way. The next one has to be this fellow O'Dea. Did you give Smiley the word on him?'

Pelly nodded. 'Couple of days ago.'

'Let's hope he does a better job there than he did on Duncan and Oliver,' put in Al Rindler.

'He damn well better,' seconded Ackerman heavily. 'He had them both dead to rights. Duncan clear sighted in a lighted doorway, and missed him clean. Oliver with his back turned on a dark night and only cut up some. That sort of bungling won't do. A dead man can be buried and quick forgotten. But those who should have been done for but are still around, and talking, can raise merry hell with us. Right now I'm not too happy with Smiley Slade, and wondering if he's worth a full share when the payoff comes.'

'Smiley's all right,' defended Pelly. 'Nobody can shoot center all the time.'

'That could be,' admitted Ackerman grudgingly. 'But we can't afford too many mistakes. Now we have this fellow Ellerson to figure out. He might be a bad one with a gun. If he is, and tied in with Scotty Duncan, that should concern you, Al.'

Rindler shifted his shoulders carelessly, spoke the same way. 'Not too much. I've looked through smoke at all kinds. Some good, some bad, some ordinary. None of them are around any more. But I am.'

Ackerman drummed restless fingers on the table top.

'You make it sound good.' To Pelly he added, 'See what true word you can get on this Ellerson, Jack. Maybe Buck Devlin could tell us something.'

Pelly nodded and went out. Ackerman waited for the door to close before speaking his next thought. 'You know, Al – our one weak angle is that our setup here is too big for just the two of us to handle all the details. We got to depend on hired hands who can slack off on us.'

Al Rindler laughed thinly. 'You worry too much, Duke. Most of the miners are sheep. They mill around, raise dust and noise, but never do anything drastic without a leader to pull them along. So we take care of the leaders, real and would-be, and the rest takes care of itself. Maybe Smiley Slade has messed up a couple of times, but he won't slack off on you. Not so long as he can see the promise of gold dust. He's one of the greediest I ever came across. Save your worries – we'll get along.'

'Providing we keep the pressure on in the right places,' Ackerman said. 'Maybe some more weight on Jim Oliver. Something to scare him and shut his mouth.'

Al Rindler nodded. 'I'll think of something.'

He went away then, softly. Almost too softly. There was ever this suggestion of cat-like stealth in all of Rindler's moves. A thing Duke Ackerman had noted before and now carefully considered again with some uneasiness. Possessing no shred of conscience himself, he doubted the existence of it in any other man.

'Sometimes I wonder, Al,' he muttered. 'Like how far any man can really be trusted. And why every now and then I get the feeling that you move around just a little too damn quiet!'

Standing in the back door of the cook shack, Ozzie Sipe beat on an iron triangle gong, sending a jangling noon meal summons all across Scotty Duncan's freight and stage compound. Over at the blacksmith shop where the mellow clangor of hammer on anvil had sounded throughout most of the morning, that echo now ceased and the brawny figure of the smith showed, stripping off his heavy leather apron. From here and there about the compound other corral and wagon hands appeared. A pair of teamsters who had been greasing one of the double hitch Merivale freight outfits, broke off that chore and joined the drift toward the wash bench beside the cookshack door.

Passing the warehouse, Cleve Ellerson found Sash Jeffers dropping in beside him with a grinning remark. 'Every time I set eyes on you, you're looking better. You seem to fill out right before a man's eyes.'

'Man either gets better – or worse,' smiled Ellerson in return. 'Happy it's the first with me.'

Jeffers laid a measuring glance on the group at the wash bench and lowered his voice. 'Buck Devlin's been making war talk. That's him with the basin, now. You watch him. He can be mean as hell.'

Ellerson laughed softly. 'Between you and Lafe Kenna you'll have me running scared unless I watch out. Of course I'm obliged, just the same.'

As he and Jeffers approached, talk in the group dwindled to a waiting quiet, as though something was expected to happen. With the next step Ellerson took, it did. The fellow with the wash basin half turned, and with a swinging throw sloshed the dirty, soapy contents of the basin across Ellerson's boots. After which a little sigh filtered through the group, while the charged silence ran.

Recalling what Scotty Duncan had said about there being a time for violence and a time for coolness and balance, Ellerson held back the quick, hot anger that surged through him. He looked down at his drenched boots, then at the lank, roan-headed Buck Devlin, who returned the glance with a mocking truculence.

Still hanging on to this feelings, Ellerson knew that in general it paid to give a trouble hunter plenty of rope and time in which to entangle and damn himself. So now, though his words were terse, they fell quietly.

'Accident – or on purpose?'

Devlin's leering challenge deepened. 'Mister, you should watch better where you're goin', or you might run into most anything. You walked right into that.'

There wasn't even a shadow of mirth in the smile Ellerson showed him. 'You could be right. Maybe I did.'

Further sneering remark shaped Buck Devlin's lips, but it was headed off when Ozzie Sipe yelled an impatient summons from the cookshack door.

'All right – all right – come alive out there! You fellers want this grub or don't you? It's on the table and I ain't leavin' it there all day. You want it – get in here …!'

Still scolding as they filed in, Ozzie gave a startled yelp as Giff Gale, the big blacksmith caught him by both arms, lifted him effortlessly and put him down in a far corner, sputtering and swearing.

'Little man,' the blacksmith chuckled, 'You're noisy as a jay bird and twice as pesky. Don't worry about the grub, we'll take care of it.'

A general laugh ran down the room and for the moment the tension eased. But Ellerson knew the pause was only temporary. A new boss always had to face a judgement, so he knew that somewhere along the line he'd have to plant his flag and make it stick.

Meanwhile, in Jim Oliver's eating house up the street, moving busily from kitchen to counter and back again, Holly Yarnell found herself throwing a quick glance every time the door swung before the push of another hungry customer, and each time she knew a twinge of disappointment when it failed to show the tall, gaunt shouldered figure of the man she had ridden the stage with from Chinese Flat.

That taciturn, still-faced man who, aside from some slight gruffness of manner, had shown her consideration and kindness. And to whom she had, in return, given only a fleeting, qualified thanks And last night, after a long and tiring day, she had lain awake in her bed, wondering why.

Going back hour by hour, incident by incident over the tumultuous day, she had finally managed to pinpoint the start of her negative reaction. It had come when he briefly explained the reason for his poor condition of affairs. There had been, it seemed, a gun fight over a poker game in some wild cattle town. When the smoke cleared away there was a gambler dead on the floor, and Cleve Ellerson was the one who had put him there.

The word of this had come almost casually. Which was what had upset her, a seeming unconcern over having shot another man to death. It had jolted her into withdrawn silence.

Later, at the scene of the stage holdup, she had seen swift change in Ellerson's attitude. There he had shown open, bitter anger over the two men lying dead, men he had never seen before. There were, apparently, certain rough standards concerning such things in this rough man's world. What counted was not so much that men died. It was how they died, and for what reason.

If she needed proof that his was such a world, there was the present condition of her brother-in-law, Jim Oliver, to provide it. So she would try to understand such standards and learn to accept them. Also, she vowed, the next time she saw Cleve Ellerson, she would show him a more generous face.

Entirely unaware of being in any way the subject of a young woman's thoughts, Ellerson sat alone at the cookshack table, leisurely finishing his noon meal. He rolled a cigarette to go along with a final cup of coffee, while sorting out the facts surrounding what undoubtedly lay immediately ahead.

He pushed away from the table and was getting to his feet when Ozzie Sipe limped over and began cleaning up.

'Probably none of my business,' the little cook observed. 'But I'm making it so. By all the signs, one thing is certain. Before you'll have firm grip on your job, you've got to beat the ears off Buck Devlin. You won't find him easy. He's a lefty and he's whipped a lot of men with that left hand. Punches coming from that side fool most men, and they don't know how to keep clear of them. Still and all, like I said, it's probably none of my business.'

'Well now, I'm glad you made it some,' Ellerson returned. 'I seem to find friends in lots of places.'

Ozzie chuckled dryly. 'Suppose I put it this way. Me, I hate Buck Devlin's guts. He's meaner than a damned rattlesnake, the sort to stomp a man, once he has him down. You watch that left hand of his'.

'Should things shape up so, I'll remember that,' said Ellerson soberly. 'And – thanks, Ozzie!'

Outside the crew was a lounging group at the corner of the bunkhouse. Buck Devlin was part of it, though standing slightly apart, watching the cookshack door. As Cleve Ellerson stepped into view, Devlin came around a little, squaring himself. Ellerson noted the move and understood it. Here it is, he told himself bleakly. But let him start …!

He moved ahead as though to pass and was in no way surprised when Devlin gave him a rough shoulder and

equally rough remark. 'There you go again, not watchin'
where you're goin'. Even bumpin' into folks. Mister, you
better start openin' your eyes before you meet up with
real trouble!'

Before leaving quarters that morning, Ellerson had
tucked his gun under his belt. Now he drew it and tossed
it to Giff Gale, the blacksmith.

'Hold that for me. I won't need it for this chore.' He
came around as he spoke and backhanded Buck Devlin
across the mouth with a cutting slash of hard knuckles.
'All right, bucko boy – you've been looking for it. Now
you've found it. Cut your God damned wolf loose ...!'

First sight of Ellerson's gun brought a quick mutter of
protest from the crew, but this quieted just as quickly
when he got rid of it. Devlin showed a flicker of trapped
dismay, which now became one of mocking anticipation.
He scrubbed a hand across his stung and bleeding lips,
droned a thin, searing curse and sidled toward Ellerson,
right fist making pawing feints, left dropped down and
back of his hip. The man was confident and dangerous.

'I'll have to end this quick!' Ellerson thought.

He shifted to face Devlin and at that move Devlin
lunged in, bringing his fist up and over and around,
grunting with the effort behind it. It was the punch
Ozzie Sipe had warned against. It was sudden, it was
fast, aimed to stun a man in his tracks – aimed to
destroy. Even though expecting it and watching for it,
Ellerson reacted barely in time by dropping his head
and hunching his right shoulder high.

Devlin's fist landed on that shoulder, rock-hard and
punishing. Then it skidded on over and caught Ellerson
high on the cheek bone under his right eye. Luckily the
shoulder had taken most of the blow, but what was left
was enough to bruise and jar Ellerson clear to his heels.
And because it had not landed as squarely as Devlin

planned, the effort he'd put behind it tipped him off balance and left his lank midriff open, his belly muscles flaccid.

Ellerson made the most of the opportunity, sinking both fists, left and right, into that open target, lifting from slightly bent knees to get all he could behind the blows. The first blasted the breath from Devlin, and then the right doubly hard, hammered home. It was wickedly calculated, savagely delivered, and it fairly lifted Devlin off his feet, numbed and weakened. Chin wobbling, mouth gaped wide he began to sag. Ellerson hooked a short left to the face, tipping Devlin's head back, his jaw loose and open. Ellerson brought his right across, rolling full weight of his shoulder behind the punch.

That finished it. Devlin reeled back into the bunkhouse wall and slid down into an awkward heap. Ellerson stood over him for a watchful moment or two before lifted a curt call. 'Bring a bucket of water, Ozzie!'

Grinning from ear to ear, Ozzie obliged. 'Just right – just right!' he chortled.

Ellerson emptied the water on Devlin, bringing him part way back to the world of harsh realities. He stared up, bleary eyed, bloody faced.

'You're fired,' Ellerson told him bluntly. 'Get your gear and yourself clear of the premises. Scotty Duncan will be back tomorrow and he'll pay you off then. Too bad it had to end this way, but you insisted on it.' He turned to Giff Gale for his gun, then ran his glance over the rest of the group. 'Apparently you wanted to find out something. Well, now you have! You all know what your jobs are. Get at them!'

He went on over to his quarters, leaving behind a subdued, wholly convinced crew of men. Giff Gale said it for all of them.

'He'll do – plenty!'

Back in quarters, Ellerson sagged down on his bunk, realizing that though he had come a long way back, he was still not completely his old self. The explosive drive he'd poured into the showdown, brief as it had been, had burned up more of his newly regained strength than he realized. Now the reaction had set in and he was content to sprawl motionless for a little time, letting the inner fires cool.

With his thoughts clearing, he pondered his position carefully. No doubt of it, Scotty was hiring that big Colt weapon under his belt.

This being the case, it behooved him to garner as much information as he could concerning the camp and the people in it. Made restless by this conviction he left the bunk, aware of a growing soreness in his cheek, up under his eye.

Outside, Ellerson went along to the Oliver eating house and with his hand on the door, paused, alertness stirring. Beyond the door a man's deep voice was rolling out angry words.

'There's no food in this place for the likes of you, Morley. Not for you or any of Duke Ackerman's crowd. That is my final word. So you can quit bully-ragging me and my women folks and get out of here with your cheap talk and threats!'

Very quietly, Ellerson opened the door and slipped through. Two men were at the counter. A third faced them, a fair-haired man, but with cheeks pale and drained and eyes sunken from some recent illness or injury. One shoulder was bulked with bandages and his arm was cradled in a sling. Beyond him, past the kitchen half wall, Helen Oliver and Holly Yarnell stood. The older woman's face was drawn and anxious. But Holly Yarnell was flushed with a hot indignation and strong anger shone in her eyes. Helen Oliver called worriedly.

'Don't argue with them, Jim. Let me feed them and get rid of them.'

'Won't be necessary, ma'am. They're leaving – now …!'

Ellerson spoke as quietly as he had entered, but the words brought Morley and his companion, the tinhorn Deuce Carmody, quickly around, Morley beginning a thick bluster.

'Now just who the hell …?'

'Shut up!' Ellerson cut him off as though using a whip. 'You were told to leave. Do it while you're able to, or it won't be just an elbow in the ribs this time. The same goes for you, tinhorn!'

They measured him carefully. Beyond the kitchen half wall, Holly Yarnell caught her breath. Here was that gaunt shouldered figure she'd been thinking about and now, hovering dangerously near the surface, she recognized that same capacity for explosive violence she'd recognized in him during the stage ride. The pair of roughs he'd laid his scalding words on saw and recognized that cold and ready purpose also, and it turned them docile and wary. Morley pocketed his gold poke and shuffled toward the door. Passing, he had his final say.

'Duke Ackerman will hear about this!'

'That's right – he will,' returned Ellerson harshly. 'I'll make it a point to tell him myself. Move out!'

When they were gone, Ellerson faced Jim Oliver. 'Good man. Don't let them push you an inch. Now, if you feel up to it, I'd like a half hour of your time.'

FIVE

'It's like this,' began Ellerson slowly. 'When I hit camp yesterday afternoon I was flat broke. Not being a miner I didn't know where or how to start. Then Scotty Duncan picked me up, thanked me for bringing in his stages and offered me a job. Some of the angles of that job seem certain to have me facing trouble. I've had a look at Scotty's side of the picture. Now I'd like your idea. Where's the real weight in this camp? What about this fellow Duke Ackerman, who seems to be top dog?'

Jim Oliver mused a moment. 'Let's start at the beginning, My wife and I and Helen's sister, Holly ran an eating house at the Granite Lake diggings. While there I grubstaked a miner named Danny Yokum, never really expecting much in return, which was to be half of anything he found. One day word came from Danny that he'd hit it rich here on Rawhide Creek, had in fact staked the Discovery claim. Helen and I left Granite Lake and set up business here. Holly was to join us later.

'Danny Yokum couldn't wait to show me over the Discovery claim. We checked corners and boundaries carefully. Overnight, Danny disappeared and Duke Ackerman moved in, contending that Danny Yokum had sold the property to him with no mention of any grubstake deal with me. I refused to swallow Ackerman's story, and on looking the claim over again I saw that the monuments and boundary stakes weren't the same as they had been when I went over the same ground with Danny. I had plenty to say about this at a miners' meeting one night, and, while on my way home from the meeting, somebody sneaked up behind me and stuck a knife in my back. Their aim wasn't quite good enough to finish me, but as you can see, it didn't do me any good. I never saw the fellow who cut me.'

'What,' asked Ellerson, 'was the miners' meeting about?'

'Mainly about Ackerman moving in on Discovery and the two rich adjoining claims, Number One above and Number One below,' Oliver explained. 'Contending that the boundaries of these were at such wide variance to their recorded descriptions, it left them open to relocation. Ned Tomlin owned Number One above and Johnny O'Dea Number One below. Naturally both raised a chunk of hell over Ackerman's steal. Now Ned Tomlin is dead and Johnny O'Dea is trying to locate pay dirt further down the flats. While Duke Ackerman has sluice boxes running from daylight to dark, looting all that good gravel.'

'There's plenty I don't know about the mining game,' Ellerson confessed. 'So I ask questions. If those claims above and below had been filed in error, would Ackerman have the legal right to relocate and move in on them?'

Jim Oliver nodded. 'If they had been. But as I say, changing the boundary stakes of Discovery would naturally throw the adjoining claims out of line.'

'You'd suggest this fellow Ackerman deliberately moved the Discovery boundaries to lay the other claims open to relocation?'

'Not suggesting,' Oliver countered with emphasis. 'I'm

saying flatly that he did. Duke Ackerman is a damned thief, and worse, surrounded by others of the same breed. His story of Danny Yokum's disappearance – of having sold to him and then gone wandering off with his burro, looking for another strike, simply doesn't go over with me. Danny was an honest man, and no fool. He had here what he'd been looking for all his life. He'd never have sold out.'

'Have you called in the law on any of this?'

Jim Oliver's short laugh was scoffing. 'What law? You mean Pelly? Hell, man – Jack Pelly is just another Ackerman bully boy, following orders. You got to say this for Ackerman – he's playing a shrewd hand. One way or another he's got about every angle sewed up tight.'

Ellerson got to his feet. 'Maybe I'll have a look to see how tight.'

On the way out he found the eating house empty except for a slim figure in gingham toiling with a mop and a bucket of steaming water. Holly Yarnell straightened, brushed back a stray lock of hair and showed him a smiling, half shy glance.

'Better,' he approved. 'Much better. Last night, when I was here with Scotty Duncan, you looked at me like I was a piece of furniture. Why the change?'

'Several things,' she answered carefully. 'One is I did not thank you properly for the kindness you showed me yesterday. So now I do. Also, I'd thank you for getting rid of that pair of roughs a little bit ago. So I wonder what it is about you that can make other men literally grovel. In a way it frightens me, even though I know you can be kind.'

Ellerson blinked. 'Am I that complicated?'

'Never mind,' she retorted. 'I know what I see. And you've been fighting again.'

'How'd you know?'

She laughed softly. 'I've seen black eyes before. You're sprouting a dandy.'

Grinning ruefully, Ellerson fingered the bruise on his cheek. 'Might have been worse. Might even have been licked.'

'At least there was no shooting, I suppose?' Her tone sobered. 'Which is something to be thankful for.'

'Just so,' Ellerson agreed. 'Who started this shooting talk, anyhow? And what's for supper tonight?'

'Elk steak, if you don't show up too late.'

'I'll be here – early. Ate breakfast and dinner with the crew. Ozzie Sipe is a top-hand cook and the crew a pretty good bunch of men. But they don't begin to rate with you when it comes to looks.'

She flushed. 'Now you're starting to get fresh and tell lies,' she accused with mock severity. 'And that is not like you, Mister Cleve Ellerson!'

He chuckled. 'Me – telling lies to you? Never! God's truth, girl – even when scrubbing a floor, you sure decorate this melancholy world. Mind you, now – make my steak a tenderloin, as I'll certainly be here after it!'

Holly Yarnell stared at the door that closed behind him, at first pensively, then slowly smiling. It was a small smile, closely held and guarded.

Warmed by the spring sunshine and the two big whiskies Cleve Ellerson bought for him, old Lafe Kenna had curled up at the foot of a convenient wall and slept the afternoon away. Now with the day running out and the shadows of a swift closing twilight flowing down from the hills, the whiskey demon was rampant again, lifting him to unsteady feet. Yonder the Lucky Lode let out a flare of early lamplight, drawing Kenna over to hover just outside the door. The crush of men thickened and Lafe Kenna peered in, watching the shift and swing of the crowd. In particular he watched Tug Morley. Looming big and beefy in a white shirt, the Lucky Lode bouncer moved about the room. Experienced at this sort of work, Morley knew that these miners, jovial and good-natured for the most part, could, on occasion when the whiskey began to take hold, turn to swift and wicked combat any moment over some slight, real or fancied. And the surest way to discourage such brawls was to put out the fires before they really got under way.

Lafe Kenna hoped to slip inside and work his way to the bar on the chance of being staked to a drink by some large-handed miner who had had a good day with his gold pan or rocker.

He watched Tug Morley make another of his rounds, saw him pause at a poker table and at the faro layout where Al Rindler held down the lookout's stool. Shifting and edging and beginning to shake a little under the whip of demanding nerves and seeing Tug Morley's back to the door, Lafe dodged inside and began working his way to the bar.

On the faro lookout's stool, Al Rindler was high enough to have full view of the room. As always, his tawny glance was forever alert, not only watching the turn of the cards and the case play on the table before him, but also roving over the shift of the crowd. So it was that during one swing of his glance he glimpsed Lafe Kenna's quick, furtive entrance.

Rindler lifted a hand, caught Tug Morley's eye and brought him over with a jerk of the head. His murmured words turned Morley swiftly around and sent him fast moving for the front of the room, bulling his way along roughly. Alerted by a miner's protesting curse at being ruthlessly shouldered aside, Lafe Kenna glimpsed the threatening approach in time to make it to

the door, but not in time to get completely clear.
Morley's reaching grab caught him just as both spun
through the door into the outer night.

'Warned you,' he snarled heavily. 'Warned you –
plenty! So now ...!'

He finished the words with a knotted fist smashing
into Kenna's face. Half stunned, the old fellow sagged.
Morley hauled him back up and held him so while
driving his fist home again and again. Kenna made
feeble effort to fight back, but there was nothing behind
it save a quick fading desperation. During these
dimming moments Kenna realized that Morley was
cursing him viciously, and also, strangely enough,
cursing Cleve Ellerson.

Limp and senseless now, Kenna had long since ceased
to feel or know anything and Morley, finally aware of
this, drove home one more blow before throwing the old
fellow aside, to lie still and shrunken against the dark
earth.

At this moment, down toward the lower end of the flats,
a miner crouched over his camp fire, cooking his
supper. It would be a late supper, as Johnny O'Dea had
worked through the last fading moments of daylight
with fruitless results. He was a sturdy chunk of a man,
round and ruddy of face, his sloping shoulders hunched
a trifle from a lifetime of work with pick and shovel and
gold pan. This day of such toil had been the poorest in
returns for him since coming to these Rawhide Creek
diggings.

The last half dozen pans he'd worked had not shown
enough color to rate mention. So, while waiting now for
his supper to heat in his dutch oven, a pot of coffee to
turn over and the loaf of bannock bread in his skillet to
swell and brown, the canker of a raw injustice gnawed at

him ceaselessly. He thought of Duke Ackerman's sluice boxes now working the rich claim that had once been his and he searched his mind over and over for a way to regain his rights.

But not Ned Tomlin's way. Robbed of his claim, Tomlin had brooded until he lost his head and made the wrong move. Now he lay dead by a slug from Al Rindler's ready gun. There was a way, the one sure way, if he could bring it about; a miners' court to take over all authority, make the necessary arrests, render fair judgment and then punish ruthlessly. That was the sure way, but it was something else to bring it about.

He well knew how variable human nature could be – how it could run hot and cold. How men could be stirred into vowing all sorts of action, but when faced with the responsibility of extreme action, how those vows could be forgotten and everything dissolve into nothing more than empty talk! Particularly could this be so when asked to take strong stand against injustice done to others than themselves.

Already, with some in camp, Ned Tomlin's death was just an item of something that had happened yesterday and therefore a regretable part of the past that could not be reversed or brought back. Meanwhile, the living had troubles and problems of their own to contend with, such as valuable time running out while gold was waiting to be dug. That, concluded Johnny O'Dea wearily, was how it was and how it would probably always be …

He lifted the top of the dutch oven, sniffed the savory contents, tucked the coffee pot deeper into the coals, and with expert touch flipped the bannock loaf over to brown the other side. And now through the deepening gloom sounded approaching footsteps and a friendly call.

'Toby Stent, Johnny. My coffee pot sprung a leak.

How's to borrow your spare for a meal? I'll return it right after I eat.'

O'Dea hunched a shoulder toward the dark bulk of his brush and canvas wickiup cabin. 'Help yourself, Tobe. It's hanging on the door post.'

Toby Stent collected the desired utensil and paused by the fire. 'What kind of day did you have?'

'Worst since I hit here.' O'Dea's reply was gruff with disgust. 'Not a single decent pan. So while I work for nothing, Duke Ackerman grows rich on a claim that is really mine.'

'Dirty damn shame,' commiserated Stent. 'Must be something you can do about it.'

'Tell me: what?' O'Dea growled. 'Go off my head like Ned Tomlin did and end up dead? Well, I'm not ready for anything like that just yet.' A cloud of steam came from the coffee pot and he lifted it aside. 'But I'm not ready to give in, either. I'll have another try at stirring up enough of the boys to show Duke Ackerman and his gang just who in hell is running this camp. Then we'll see!'

'That's it,' agreed Toby Stent. 'A miners' court, some rope and a handy tree will fix things. It's been done before.'

He went away then. Johnny O'Dea poured his coffee, halved the hot, crunchy bannock loaf, spooned up his supper and ate with a hungry man's gusty satisfaction. The hot food was a stimulant to pick him up, lighten his weariness, steady his mood. He would, he decided, call on Jim Oliver tomorrow and see what suggestions he had to offer. This idea was something to muse over while he loaded his pipe with navy rough cut. With the pipe alight and drawing freely he settled back to savor this good half hour of peace and quiet while night laid on its blanket of velvet dark ever deeper.

The fire burned down to a core of ruddy coals that glowed through a coating of graying ash. Then even these, one by one, snapped and broke apart and became just another fragment of ash stirring slightly before the push of the small wind that winnowed along the flats. Given time, there was, it seemed, an end to all things. Even the eternal fire could burn out and die.

Again came the shuffle of approaching steps. Lounging in this full comfort, intent on his thoughts, Johnny O'Dea neither turned or looked. It would be, he decided, Toby Stent returning the borrowed coffee pot, so he offered lazy direction.

'Just hang it where you found it, Tobe.'

But the approaching steps did not stop at the cabin. They came right on up to the fire, and now, with purely animal alarm whipping all through him, Johnny O'Dea sensed the threat of the broad, squat figure looming over him.

He tried to lunge upright. He never got there. A down-sweeping forearm, hard and heavy as a slab of oak, slashed across his throat, driving back any cry of alarm and spinning him face down into the fire ash. Bunched knees landed heavily on the small of his back, pinning him. Then a heavy, murderous blade swept up and down – up and down, driving deep – deep ...!

Johnny O'Dea shuddered, gasped once, then made no further sound or move ...

It was full sundown when Cleve Ellerson again stepped into the Oliver eating house. He had spent the afternoon in the compound and warehouse, familiarizing himself with all the layout and its necessary activities. Also testing the mood of the crew and happily finding it good. Buck Devlin was gone, a fact Ozzie Sipe remarked on with open satisfaction. 'And,' Ozzie added, 'wherever he is, I hope he's in misery. Because he's one mean bastard and deserves nothin' better.'

The eating house was crowded and Ellerson had to wait for some little time before finding place at the counter. Beyond the kitchen partition Helen Oliver hovered over the big cooking range, while behind the counter Holly Yarnell moved swiftly back and forth, feeding the hungry. When she put Ellerson's supper before him, a faint lift of her lip's corners and a soft shine in her eyes broke the cloak of strict impartiality she'd shown the balance of the room.

In response, Ellerson knew a gust of pleasure that surprised him. How long, he mused, since a personable young woman had shown him any expression of favor? And since when had he really given a damn whether one did or not? For so long had his world been strictly a man's world, wherein it seemed every man's hand was spread against every other man's hand, a jungle in which men fought with and preyed upon each other with little, if any, mercy. A time of hard riding, ruthless days with the raw breath of powder smoke in the air and the simple fact of mere existence boiled down to the law of the fang. When most of the past was full of dark shadows and the future a time of complete uncertainty; wild, uncaring days through which a man lived his harsh and reckless hours, wondering when and if the final roll of the dice of fate would come up wrong ...

Such were the days of the Tarpe Grant range war, and before that the days of similar wars on other ranges. When a man was young and wild and full of hell, and his gun was for sale to the highest bidder, and nothing was of any account save the challenge and the danger and the hard-won respect of other men as wild and heedless as himself.

That was how it was then, and why should it be

different now? Why had there been a change, and where and when had that change taken place? It must have been, he decided soberly, during the misery days and weeks in that bleak, cheerless hotel room in Border City while waiting for his wounded side to heal and when no one – not even the doctor who mended him – seemed overly concerned if he lived or died.

Throughout the dismal monotony of such empty, lonely moments a man could do a lot of thinking, toting up the bankrupt past and pondering the equally bankrupt possibilities of the future. And if he found the values hopelessly meager and had the courage and good sense to admit them, then he was bound to see himself in a clear and merciless light. After which it meant making some drastic changes for the better, or writing himself off completely as a useful member of the human race.

Immersed in such gray thoughts he had eaten mechanically and slowly and now his plate lay empty before him. But only for a moment until a generous slice of raisin pie slid on to it, accompanied by the soft fall of quiet words.

'You might like this better than you did the rest of your supper.'

He looked up to meet Holly Yarnell's concerned glance. The crowd had thinned out, only a couple of miners still holding place at the far end of the counter. He spoke his quick protest.

'The supper was great – every bite of it. But I can't say as much for some of the thoughts I was chewing on.'

'I knew something was wrong,' she said gently. 'You were such a long way off.'

'That I was,' he agreed. 'Flat on my back in a cheap hotel room in Border City. There was nothing in that room but me and about two hundred flies. I know there were that many because I counted them. I bet I counted

those damn flies near a hundred times. It helped to ride
out the time. The sawbones who sewed me up knew his
professional business, all right, but beyond that he could
have passed as a wooden Indian.

'The hotel flunky who brought me what he called
food, chewed snuff and let it dribble. He also had dirty
finger nails. All of which I wouldn't have minded in a
branding corral, but not while handling my grub.
Something happened to me during that time, a change
of some kind, and I've been trying to figure out just
what it was and if I'm set for a better deal than the old
one was.' He shrugged, grinning wryly. 'I sure was glad
to get shot of that bed and that room.'

Charged with sympathy, Holly Yarnell's eyes were
very soft. Her words were equally gentle.

'The past hasn't treated you very well, has it?'

'The past,' he differed gruffly, 'has been entirely of
my own making. If any scars are left, I can blame no one
but myself.'

Looking at her, he marveled at how fair she stood in
his eyes. Pure impulse swayed him again, coloring his
words. 'Girl, I'm a poor hand at saying such things. But
this I said before and must say it again. When you are in
a room it takes on a glow!'

Eyes wide and startled, confusion staining her cheeks,
she stammered breathlessly. 'That, from you – from
you! Now, how can I ask you to pay for your supper …?'

She didn't try. Cheeks afire, she scurried back into the
kitchen.

Wondering wryly at himself, Ellerson finished his pie,
spun up a cigarette, laid a dollar beside his empty plate
and went out into the night. First thought had been to
return to quarters and an early bed. But now there was a
restlessness that turned him up street, testing the sounds
and sights of the night. Big and luminous against their

black vault the stars bloomed, their radiance silvering roof tops and the empty run of the street. On either hand the hills reared, massive, eternal, in a night so still the tireless rush of the creek waters lifted clearly above all else, a peaceful, soothing sound.

Now, abruptly, came another sound, starting far down on the flats, but carrying nearer and nearer as one voice picked it up and passed it on to another. It was a human crying, so wild and charged with bitter anger that at first it held no coherent meaning. But it came on and on until finally its dark and brutal substance became clear.

'He's dead! Johnny O'Dea – is dead! Johnny O'Dea – knifed in the back ...'

Ever too realistic in his thinking to know superstition of any kind, Cleve Ellerson had never seen anything particularly mysterious in the hard, barren facts of life. Men lived and men died, some peacefuly in their beds, some violently out along the far edges of a rough world. Yet, at this time and in these surroundings, that wailing cry was a dread and dismal sound.

'Johnny O'Dea – he's dead! He's been knifed ...!'

These final words stopped Ellerson in his tracks. Short hours before he had listened to a man who had known the bite of treacherous steel. Jim Oliver, who told of three men who dared to publicly charge that they had been robbed. One was Oliver himself. The others were Johnny O'Dea and Ned Tomlin. Now both were dead. Only Jim Oliver had managed to beat the odds. Also, not to be forgotten was the bullet hole in the wall of Scotty Duncan's quarters, nor the significance that lay behind it. This damn camp apparently could be a death trap for any man who dared speak his mind ...

Turning into a pocket of deep shadow at the corner of Peter Yost's trading post, Ellerson listened to the somber message of death run full length of the flats before dashing back and quieting like a spent wave. But now, from up street came further sound, the shuffle of uncertain steps, gradually nearing. Through the starlight's pale glow appeared a weaving, stumbling figure, mumbling half-groaned words.

'Morley did it – to me. Kicked hell – out of me! Like I – was – stray dog. Now can't see – hardly. And damn world's goin' round – goin' round–!'

Words and strength running out, Lafe Kenna went down in a loose sprawl.

SIX

Carrying a basin of hot water in one hand and some towels in the other, Ozzie Sipe expressed himself with considerable emphasis.

'That damn Tug Morley! Manhandlin' a poor old feller like this. Why would he do it?'

They had Lafe Kenna laid out on the floor of Ozzie's kitchen. Cleve Ellerson had brought him in, jackknifed over one shoulder. Now, with old Lafe stripped to the waist, they judged the extent of his hurts and tended them as best they could. Ellerson dipped a towel in the steaming water, wrung it out and laid the compress over Kenna's mauled face.

'Hot coffee, Ozzie,' directed Ellerson, 'and add in a good jolt of whiskey.'

They propped Kenna up, got some of the coffee and whiskey into him and he began coming around. Both eyes were swollen shut and the first words he managed were about his eyes.

'Can't see – damned thing. Where am I? Who – what–?'

'Easy does it, Lafe,' Ellerson soothed. 'You're with friends. It was Tug Morley who did this to you?'

'That's it – Morley. Beat the hell out of me and tried to kick my ribs in when I was down. Got – more of that coffee?'

'All you want.'

Once he made turn for the better, the old man came along fast. Thin and wasted as he was physically, deep down lingered a wiry toughness built up by the early good years of his life and which the later, useless ones had not completely destroyed. With returning vigor his mind quickened and his anger stirred.

'I'll get even,' he declared, between gulps of hot coffee and whiskey. 'Get even with Duke Ackerman, too. I was good enough once to earn drinks by runnin' errands for Ackerman. Then he threw me out, didn't want me anywhere around his damn deadfall. But more'n once when they didn't know I was close, I heard them talkin' about this and that. So I know more'n they think. Mebbe I *am* the worthless old dog Al Rindler called me, but I can hurt that gang!'

'I bet you can,' Ellerson said. 'We'll get at that, later.'

He looked up and made the gesture of pouring from a bottle. Ozzie Sipe grinned and mixed another cupful, this time with very little coffee and a great deal of whiskey. By the time all this was inside him, Kenna was mumbling thickly.

'Sure good to have friends – somewhere. Man'd be in – hell of a shape – without any friends at all ...'

By the time they had him cleaned up he was almost asleep. Ellerson looked him over with satisfaction.

'Had to knock him out with something. All we had was whiskey.'

'Where we goin' to put him?' Ozzie asked. 'Can't leave him here for me to stumble over.'

'For tonight,' Ellerson said, 'Scotty Duncan's bunk is empty. That should do.'

They hoisted Kenna to stumbling feet and half steered, half carried him out and around and inside again to Scotty's bunk. Even as they laid him down he began to snore.

Ozzie chuckled. 'Should keep until morning all right. That last jolt I poured was damn near straight liquor, and it was a big one. Ordinary man'd been knocked cold for a week, but this old jigger's been years buildin' up a capacity for the stuff. Damn, he sure was worked over, wasn't he? Come mornin' he'll be too stiff and sore to wiggle. I'll see he gets a good breakfast.'

Ozzie headed back to his kitchen and Ellerson, spreading a blanket over the huddled figure on the bunk, knew a twinge of conscience. This whole thing could be mainly his fault. In buying the two drinks for Kenna in the Lucky Lode earlier in the day, he had antagonized Tug Morley, and, afraid to strike back directly, Morley had taken out his venom on old Lafe.

Ellerson carried the acceptance of guilt with him when he went to bed, which confirmed how definitely he was becoming committed against certain elements of this camp. Not merely because he had taken on with Scotty Duncan, but because fate had a way of entangling a man in a web of circumstances and challenges he couldn't back away from, not if he hoped to maintain any decent opinion of himself. One way or another he accumulated debts that had to be repaid before the books stood cleared and a balance struck. He could only accept the cards dealt him and play them accordingly.

On this summation of the situation he slept.

He was up, dressed and had a fire going when Ozzie Sipe, good to his word, limped in with breakfast for Lafe Kenna. It took a little urging to bring Kenna around, but cold water, then a drying towel across his bruise blackened face did the trick. He grunted and groaned and grumbled protesting curses. But presently, after getting outside of some coffee laced with whiskey, he took stock, blinking around with one eye barely open between puffed lids.

'Ain't rightly sure where I am or how I got here,' he mumbled, peering up at Ellerson. 'But I remember you, You're the feller who bought me drinks in the Lucky Lode?'

Ellerson nodded. 'That's right. Name's Ellerson.'

Kenna blinked thoughtfully, something stirring in his confused thoughts. 'Ellerson,' he mumbled. 'Ellerson. Now there's an odd thing. When Tug Morley was maulin' and cussin' me, he was cussin' the name of Ellerson, too. Why do you think that was?'

'Think I know,' Ellerson said. 'Later on, I'll explain. Just now, let's get some food into you.'

Once started, Lafe Kenna ate and drank eagerly. Finished, he settled back with a sigh. 'You're sure one good feller, Ellerson.'

'Then how's to answer some questions for me?'

'Do my best. What'cha want to know?'

'Last night you said something about getting even with certain people. Said you'd listened to their talk and knew more about their affairs than they realized. What was it you meant?'

Kenna hesitated gathering his thoughts. 'Mebbe it don't amount to as much as I thought. Somewhere around here in the hills is a cabin. Some horses coraled there, too, along with a lot of ridin' gear for a fast getaway, should one come up necessary. And one of Ackerman's crowd hangs out there.'

'Fast getaway from what – and why?' Ellerson asked.

Kenna shook his head slowly. 'All I know is I heard Duke Ackerman say that a fast getaway might be necessary, some day.'

'Who is it that hangs out at this cabin?'

'Ain't never seen him,' Kenna admitted. 'But I heard

'em call him Smiley.'

Ellerson started slightly, his eyes pinching down. 'Smiley, eh? Not a common tag. Smiley – who?'

Again Kenna wagged his head. 'Since that clubbin' I took from Morley I ain't thinkin' too good. Lemme see, now ... ! Smiley – Smiley ...?' His mauled features took on a gargoyle scowl of concentration. 'Wait a minute – I think I got it! Slade – that's it – Smiley Slade!' Noting the expression that pulled at Ellerson's cheeks, he exclaimed further. 'What the hell – would you be knowin' him?'

'A chance – a thin one,' Ellerson said carefully. 'But once I knew of a Smiley Slade. Long way from here, though.'

'Man never knows,' Lafe said. 'People move around, everybody follerin' a trail of some kind. And trails could cross.'

'True enough,' Ellerson agreed. 'Lafe, this earns you another drink.'

Kenna put the drink away, then flattened out on the bunk. 'Feelin' better – just a hell of a lot better – though I could use a little more sleep.'

'All you want,' Ellerson said moving to the door. 'And – thanks!'

The crew had finished and left by the time Ellerson reached the cook shack for his breakfast, so he had the place to himself. Stirred by what Lafe Kenna had told him, memories of the wild days of the Tarpe Grant range war and of the men who rode through them, came flooding back. He himself had been one of those men. Among the others had been one named Slade, known to his fellows as Smiley.

A strange-shaped man, as Ellerson remembered, long of body on short, bowed legs, with dangling, ropey arms, and who always moved in a sort of half-crouch. A man whose appearance hinted of the simian, with a thick nostriled nose and a mouthful of heavy teeth in a grimace that passed for a smile. It was because of this that the tag of Smiley was hung on him. An acquisitive man to a fantastic degree. No other rider of the outfit owned a warbag so stuffed to overflowing with trivia of doubtful, if any value. Smiley Slade had never wholly discarded anything – not even an empty Durham tobacco sack.

Strange too, mused Ellerson, how memory, when once awakened, could return so clearly the image of a man and all the happenings of a period of the past once put well behind and hopefully forgotten. Yet now, with the image of Smiley Slade before him, came all the rest of a grimly depressing picture.

A poker game in Stack Kinnard's bunkhouse had run all day, all night, and all of the following day. The play had finally worked down through the entire outfit until it became two-handed stud between Smiley Slade and Cappie Jenkins, an old horse-wrangler Stack Kinnard kept on about the place to do odd jobs. When the outfit turned in that second night, the best part of six hundred dollars was stowed away in the warbag of Cappie Jenkins.

About a week later, after a long night of hard riding and fighting that had scattered the crew widely, the active members returned to headquarters in the chill, half-disclosing light of early dawn to find Cappie Jenkins cold and dead in his bunk. He'd been knifed to death and his looted warbag lay on the bunkhouse floor beside him. While Smiley Slade was nowhere to be found ...

There had been some bursting, savage anger, along with well-meant threats among the balance of the crew at Cappie Jenkins. There had been neither time nor opportunity to mount any real pursuit of Smiley Slade.

So Cappie Jenkins was buried, his grave marked and the muffling blanket of time had turned the thoughts and purposes of men to other and more demanding issues still directly before them.

While recalling all these churning memories, Cleve Ellerson had finished eating and now was shaping up a Durham cigarette when Sash Jeffers came in, raided Ozzie Sipe's coffee pot for a cupful and sat down across from Ellerson.

'Took a jaunt around camp, judging the reaction over the knifing of Johnny O'Dea, last night. Lot of people mad enough to knock Duke Ackerman's sluice boxes to pieces, but not mad enough to go on from there. Which is aside from the question. What I figured would really interest you, is who I saw, acting real confidential and friendly like. Give you one guess.'

Ellerson smiled faintly through the upcurling smoke of his cigarette. 'Can't imagine. You tell me.'

'Jack Pelly and your late waltzing partner, Buck Devlin. What do you think?'

'While I'm trying to, let's have your ideas.'

'Like this,' Jeffers said. 'Right along we've been sending out some gold on every stage. Not too much at a time, Scotty figuring to hold down chance of a heavy loss, should a holdup take place. No sign of trouble. But the gold kept piling up until we had to send out a big shipment. We kept quiet about it. Only five people had any idea what was going out. Scotty, me, Pony Bob McCart, Jake Rivers and – Buck Devlin.

'So comes the holdup, leaving Pony Bob and Rivers dead. Somebody had talked. Certainly Scotty wouldn't and I know I didn't. Seems reasonable to doubt Pony Bob or Jake Rivers would, as it was their responsibility to get the stuff safely through. All of which leaves – who?'

Ellerson scrubbed a thoughtful hand across his chin.

'Narrows it down, for a fact. And now friend Devlin is playing it cheek by jowl with our estimable sheriff, Jack Pelly. Well and well! Wish I'd known something of this before. I'd have worked on Devlin until he talked. Maybe I still will if he's around when Scotty gets back.'

'Just so,' Jeffers approved, draining his cup and getting to his feet. He eyed Ellerson for an intent moment. 'More and more I realize why Scotty hired you on. He's one shrewd Scotsman.'

'Me,' said Ellerson wryly, 'I'm wondering if I'm up to the job.'

At the door, Jeffers paused. 'Right off the cuff, I'd say you were making a pretty good start.'

Up street, turned moody and uneasy over the rising tide of hostility and suspicion he'd encountered during an early swing around camp, Jack Pelly stepped from morning's bright sun into the murky shadow and sour odors of the Lucky Lode. But for Tug Morley, a bartender and Ace Carmody, the house tinhorn, the place was empty. Morley and the bartender were wielding brooms, mucking out the dirt and cold refuse left by last night's crowd. Alone at a poker table, Carmody was dealing showdown hands of stud. Tug Morley straightened his back and grunted a question which got him no answer as Pelly went straight on into Duke Ackerman's back office room.

With Ackerman was Al Rindler, looking sulky, while Ackerman's florid cheeks were heated. Together with the rancid smoke of Ackerman's stale and badly chewed cigar, remnants of argument hung in the air. The glance Ackerman laid on Pelly was sharp and demanding.

'Locate Devlin?'

Pelly nodded.

'Sound him out?'

Again Pelly nodded. 'But right now he's scared, Duke. That fellow Ellerson must have whipped hell out of him. Also, according to what Devlin claimed, Ellerson was packing a gun. So it strikes me that what I said before was right – Scotty Duncan has hired him a real tough hand in Ellerson.'

Ackerman waved a beefy, impatient fist. 'What I want to know – will Devlin have a try at him?'

Pelly shrugged. 'Can't say for sure. Not right away, but maybe later, if the ante is big enough and we give him time to get some salt back in his spine.'

'How much time?' Al Rindler demanded. 'How much time have we got? And can we afford to wait? Maybe we should call in Smiley Slade for that job.'

Ackerman exploded angrily. 'Not that dumb, damn animal! When he missed out on both Duncan and Jim Oliver, I told you he wouldn't do. But you were so sure he would take care of O'Dea right. To me that meant more than just sticking a knife in him and leaving him for the first passerby to stumble over. So now our sluices are in splinters, a rich clean-up gone right back into the gravel it came from, and a mad camp ready to raise hell with us. Yeah, I'm pretty weary of Smiley Slade. We'll try to bring Devlin along. Or maybe you'd like to try *your* luck?'

Instantly affronted, Rindler's pale eyes flickered. 'That's damn fool talk. Duke – and you know it! When I go after a man, I don't sneak around in the dark. I'm looking at him when I call him. You hear me – that was damn fool talk! And I don't want any more of it!'

Ackerman tossed a placating hand. 'Call it so, and forget it. We're all edgy and talking wild. If we can get Devlin to manage it, then nobody can point at us. They'll see it as him getting back at Ellerson for that licking.'

Outside the argument and not liking any part of it, Pelly asked: 'What's for me, now?'

'Get out of sight and take it easy for the rest of today. But hit the flats tomorrow and make a show of working hard at getting a line on O'Dea's killer. Ask questions. Look the ground over. Find out if anybody knows anything for sure, outside the fact that O'Dea is done for. After you get through with the flats, ride out to the cabin, see how things are there, and tell Slade I want to see him.'

'Might be smarter to keep out of sight and play it quiet for several days,' Pelly suggested. 'The feeling about us around camp ain't a bit good.'

Again Ackerman waved a placating hand. 'I'll be the judge of that. And I'm not about to stampede just yet. We'll ride this thing out. I'll have Riordan pour extra heavy drinks across the bar and make the free lunch extra generous. Most of the miners got no personal gripe against us. They're washing out enough color to keep them reasonably happy. So we keep their bellies warm and full with plenty of whiskey and free grub and they'll quiet down again.'

Dark-browed and secretive, Jack Pelly left. Never a sound man, he had long prowled the fringes of camps such as this one, alert to the best spot to catch on, always testing the odds and playing his politics carefully and to the best advantage of himself and himself only. Not as tough as his hard-faced swarthiness suggested, and governed by a calculating caution that kept him from ever committing himself completely to any cause or any other person. Always there must be a loophole for a way out, for escape, should the odds come up wrong.

Carved indelibly in his memory was an incident of a few years past in another boom camp. There he had been spectator at a miners' court wherein, with remorseless but completely fair judgement, a pair of wild ones had been tried and convicted and hanged for the murder and robbery of better men. It was a thing he had not forgotten and never would. So now he sought his cabin at the edge of camp. There he would be out of sight and sound. There, too, was a bottle to keep him company.

Back in the Lucky Lode, after an interval of thoughtful quiet, Duke Ackerman lit a fresh cigar and surveyed Al Rindler through the smoke with milder glance.

'Let's agree we've both made mistakes, Al. And we've got too much at stake here to start losing our heads. Maybe the feeling around camp is running a little high. But O'Dea was our most dangerous trouble maker – the one leader the rest of the miners were most likely to follow. Now we're rid of him. By tomorrow he'll be just another stray, dead and buried and soon to be forgotten. In the meantime we play it quiet and easy. When things simmer down, and they will, we'll build new sluices and be back in business again. Right?'

Rindler nodded. 'It's the way I'd play it,' he agreed. 'The time to press your luck is when the stakes are big enough to matter and the cards running your way. We'd be fools to figure otherwise.'

Ackerman reached for bottle and glasses. 'Let's have a drink or two on that.'

His breakfast done with, Cleve Ellerson took his cigarette and thoughts out into the day's brightness. The flats were the usual hive of activity. Somewhere someone was swinging an axe against a piece of stubborn timber and each stroke beat up a sharp echo. A double-hitch freight outfit rolled its ponderous way out of the compound and headed for the road and a run across the summit to Chinese Flat. Also catching Ellerson's swinging glance was a slim figure in gingham crossing from the eating house to Peter Yost's trading post with a market basket on her arm. Ellerson took a final drag at his cigarette, pinched out the butt, spun it away and followed her.

By the time Peter Yost finished stacking Holly Yarnell's basket it was piled high and heavy. Ellerson stepped forward and lifted it from the counter.

'Let me.'

She nodded and led the way out, color touching her cheeks. She carried herself very straight and her expression was sober and reserved. 'The day,' Ellerson drawled, as they emerged into it, 'is such a fine one it should be easy for a lady to smile.'

Her head reached no higher than his shoulder. She looked up, speaking with some severity. 'After last night, it just isn't easy to smile.'

'If what I said to you then makes you feel that way, I'll be sure not to offend again,' he observed carefully.

Her expression softened and she scolded gently. 'Don't be silly! No woman in her right mind would ever resent as nice a thing as you said to me. It's something else that haunts me. It's that – that awful thing about a miner who was stabbed to death.'

Ellerson was sympathetic. 'Dirty business, all right. Enough to upset anybody.'

She gave a little shudder. 'It's horrible! Sister Helen and I – we hardly slept after hearing of it. Because it might have been that way with our Jim. What kind of two-legged beasts roam this camp anyhow? If this is what gold does to men, then I hate the stuff!'

'Turns some savage, for a fact,' he agreed. 'There's always some mean ones to do the mean things. Still and all, there's no use getting too worked up over things you can't help or do anything about.'

She tossed a defiant head. 'If I were a man, I'd do

something!'

'Such as–?'

'I would,' she declared with a small show of fierceness, 'round up those responsible and then – then–!' Her words frittered out as the picture they were leading to became frightening and out of control.

'Sure,' Ellerson drawled, 'and then – what? Hang them to a high tree and watch them kick? That could be one of life's unpleasant moments, too – even if necessary and the right thing to do.'

She stopped and faced him, head back, eyes flashing. 'Do you have to be so – so bald about it? I – I'm no executioner!'

'Now I'm real certain of that.' A glint of fleeting amusement narrowed Ellerson's eyes. 'Instead, suppose we say just a very honest person, with spunk enough to speak her honest mind.'

She looked at him with some uncertainty. 'Would you, by any chance, be poking fun at me?'

'Never,' he vowed. 'Only after a smile from a pretty girl on a pretty morning.'

She tossed her head and went on, not facing him again until they reached the eating house door and she turned to take over her basket. Now there was a gentle, dawning smile to reward him.

'You are right, Cleve. It is a pretty morning. Thanks for reminding me.'

Moving on up street, Ellerson's musings were warm and good. These few moments with Holly Yarnell had been a pleasant interlude to brighten his day, put it in balance, and, for a little time at least, clear his mind of the dark memories he'd dredged out of the shadowed past. But now those memories returned.

Smiley Slade! Who had knifed a fellow rider while he slept. Now, so Lafe Kenna claimed, there was a Smiley

Slade somewhere in these hills. Could it be the same
one? Not likely, yet not too unlikely, either, because it
was as Ozzie Sipe had declared; the trails of men could
cross, when and where least expected. At times the
world could be very small indeed. And if it were the
same Smiley Slade, wielding here that same treacherous
knife, what would be his purpose unless under orders
and in the service of another man?

Who would be the one to benefit most from the
deaths of men like Jim Oliver and this miner, Johnny
O'Dea? From the deaths of two other miners, Ned
Tomlin and Danny Yokum? Also those of Pony Bob
McCart and Jake Rivers during the stage holdup? And
finally, what about the attempt against Scotty Duncan, a
cowardly slug from the dark that had barely missed?

There was, of course, only one answer. It was the man
Jim Oliver had named and flatly accused, the one Scotty
Duncan had also named and warned him against. The
evil of this camp was grounded in the Lucky Lode. And
how deeply did it concern him? This thought brought
him to a halt, a tall and still-faced man, his cold-eyed
glance searching the street, marking its careless disorder
and its ugliness.

What did he owe this camp, this tawdry sprawl born of
man's greed and lust for yellow wealth? Born overnight
and in all likelihood fated to die just as quickly when the
gold played out. Left would be only a scatter of stray
rubbish, a rotting wall or two, and a few scars against the
earth's patient face. Beyond that, nothing; for, given a
little time, nature would cover up even these ugly relics.
So what did he, or any other man for that matter, owe to
such a monument of tawdry impermanence?

Shoulders made restless by the insistent proddings of
his dissatisfaction and his thoughts, swung and twisted.
Had the last been the only question demanding answer,

the choice would have been simple. The hell of it was, however, it wasn't merely a matter of substance and geography. There were people to be considered. Also, there was his own self-respect. Out of a tangle of events and conditions not entirely of his own making, a challenge had reared its head. Either he must turn his back on that challenge and avoid it entirely, or he must face it and see it through, regardless.

The first meant dragging self-respect in the dirt and betraying the trust of people who did not deserve to be betrayed. No one had forced him to take on the job Scotty Duncan had offered, but, when he did, it bound him to something he could not deny or back away from. Also, how about that soft-eyed, gently smiling girl he'd just left?

Yeah, how about Holly Yarnell and her sister and her sister's husband, a man still weak and sick because of a cowardly night attack? It was not necessary to feel yourself your brother's keeper to know outrage against brutal death or treatment; you had only to recognize the call of one decent person to another.

So there was the challenge. He'd never backed away from one before, so why in hell was he even considering the thought now? There were all kinds of values mixed up here, but only the good ones should count. Again he swung his shoulders. To stand straight up in this affair, he knew what he had to do. He had to face this fellow Duke Ackerman and lay hard facts before him. He'd laid eyes on the man just once before, right after Ned Tomlin lay dead on the floor of the Lucky Lode. A big, florid-faced blustering man, as Ellerson remembered.

It would not be only Ackerman himself to convince. There was sure to be that cat-eyed, cat-footed killer, Al Rindler, and perhaps it didn't matter. ... Under his belt the bulk of the big Colt .45 gun was a pressure and a

weight against his body. And if there was any business
that he knew better than any other, it was the business of
guns. If this had not been so during the wild, early
years, then he would not be standing here, this day.

There had been some close calls, of course, but only
when he had tried to play the game softly. The last time
he had made that mistake was with the tinhorn in
Border City, and because of it had taken a derringer
slug in the ribs. So he would not make that mistake
again. If a showdown had to be called, he'd go at it the
right way, putting the pressure on the other side. Startle
them, catch them off guard, knock them off balance.
Make them guess while they tried to figure the odds and
the percentage of chance. Doing it that way, you turned
them cautious, and you held the edge because their own
fears slowed them and made them uncertain.

Further movment up street caught his eye and he
watched Jack Pelly dodge from the Lucky Lode and
angle away toward a cabin up the far slope. Well, that
made it one less to consider, and the time was now …!

The gust of feeling that brushed along Cleve
Ellerson's nerve ends was like a thin, cold deeply vital
wind cutting all through him, keening his every sense to
the finest edge. Too, it brought about the old,
well-remembered excitement that turned him at once
reckless and charged with the edge of sure purpose.
Quickly he wheeled and strode along to the Lucky Lode.

SEVEN

In the Lucky Lode, Riordan and Tug Morley had laid aside their brooms. Riordan was back in his favorite territory, polishing glasses. With a foot hoisted on a handy chair, Morley leaned an elbow on his knee and idly watched the turn of the cards as Carmody laid them down. Riordan was the first to glimpse Cleve Ellerson as he entered and was immediately fixed with a raking glance and curt order.

'You, keep polishing! I want to see your hands always in sight.'

Tug Morley jerked around with a show of surly truculence. Carmody pulled up straighter in his chair, a card hanging in hesitant fingers. Ellerson's words here were hard and sardonic.

'Go ahead, Carmody – play it! So far, you're in the clear. Be smart and stay that way. Morley, you've an accounting coming. I don't take kindly to a second-hand beating.'

Morley blinked, growling. 'Mister, in case you didn't know it, you're way off the reservation when you come in here. What the hell are you drivin' at?'

'You'll find out – all in good time,' Ellerson shot back. 'Where's Ackerman – in there?' A stabbing forefinger indicated the inner door. 'I want a talk with that fellow.'

'He's there,' Morley blustered, 'but nobody goes in there unless either Al Rindler or I say so. And you – stay out!'

Ellerson's laugh was as cold as his glance. 'You'll never stop me – now or any other time!'

He moved straight to the door, pushed it open and stepped through, quick-closing the door behind him, leaving Morley to stare, while trying to sneer down his startled discomfiture. 'Big talk – big mouth. He'll come out faster than he went in – if he's lucky!'

'Don't be a fool, Tug,' advised Carmody tensely. 'No big talk there – no bluff, either. Just danger, a lot of it and a mile high! I've seen his kind before. That man is cocked and primed for anything. In your boots, I'd walk careful and sing soft!'

In the back room, shoulders squared against the closed door, Cleve Ellerson watched with cold amusement the startled consternation his abrupt entrance had caused. Both Ackerman and Al Rindler had been lying far back at ease in their chairs, Rindler with crossed ankles propped up on the edge of Ackerman's table. Each held well-charged whiskey glasses in their right hands. Ackerman also had a cigar in the fingers of his left and was gesturing with it.

For a long, breathless second, sheer unbelieving amazement held both of them motionless. Then Rindler let out an exclamation like a muffled hiss, dropped his feet to the floor and started to turn. Ellerson stopped the move with whiplash words.

'Far enough, Rindler! Keep on nuzzling that drink while I lay a few facts of life in front of your boss. You heard me – far enough!'

Rindler heeded the warning, going completely still except for a turn of his head, his eyes going round and flat with a quick, tawny glitter. Duke Ackerman finally found voice and used it in something close to a blurting yell.

'You got a hell of a nerve, bustin' in here this way! Who the hell are you and what do you want?'

Ellerson grinned mockingly, 'The name is Ellerson. I'm Scotty Duncan's new yard boss, and I bring you a few words of gospel. Should you have ideas about sticking your nose into any of Scotty's affairs, personal or business – get rid of them! And there better be no more shots from the dark, even if they do miss. Otherwise I'll hold you strictly responsible and act accordingly. Understood?'

Ackerman's protuberant eyes bulged still more as though he could hardly believe what he saw or heard. His mouth opened and closed soundlessly as he sought for an answer. Though he had directed his talk mainly at Ackerman, it was Al Rindler who drew most of Ellerson's wire-fine alertness. It was this fellow Rindler who would harbor a relentless hostility and who could, at any treacherous second, explode into deadly action.

Ackerman gulped, cleared his throat harshly and found his voice again. 'You must be crazy! There's no quarrel between Scotty Duncan and me – no quarrel at all!'

'Somebody,' said Ellerson sententiously, 'took a shot at Scotty the other night. They didn't hit him, but it wasn't for lack of trying. Now would you know anything about that?'

'Why would I? I told you I had no quarrel with Duncan.'

A cynical lift to Ellerson's lip corners gave Ackerman the lie. 'Then there's another thing,' he went on, 'another of a lot of things. Concerns friends of mine – good people, too. Meaning Jim Oliver and his women folks. Decent folks out to make an honest living in an

honest business. Same thing goes for them as goes for
Scotty. Leave them alone, Ackerman. You and all your
crowd – leave those people alone! Anything happens to
them – anything at all – then I come after you –
personal! *Compre* ...?'

With the first shock of Ellerson's abrupt entrance and
manner and equally abrupt words now beginning to
wear off a little, change came over Duke Ackerman. His
bulgy eyes turned flat and brutal and the pull of feeling
in his florid cheeks turned his face hard and bony. And
his words turned vicious.

'You're crazy, or drunk, or both. And nobody throws
their weight around in this room and threatens me.'

'I'm here,' Ellerson reminded softly. 'And throwing
my weight around. So what?'

'Get the hell out while you're able to!' Again
Ackerman was near to yelling his anger. 'You hear me?
Get out or I'll turn Al loose on you!'

The look Ackerman now flashed at Al Rindler was
loaded with dark meaning. Reading the look and the
savage intent it carried, Ellerson laughed softly and laid
out his challenge.

'How about it, Rindler? You just got your orders. Fly
to it if you think you can get there. You've been itching
to try, and you'll never have a better chance!'

It was that bare and harsh and it caught Al Rindler off
balance, calling for a decision he was not entirely
prepared for. The thought had been with him right
along, but the stark question of yes or no had not turned
steady and solid; a thread of indecision was persistently
there. In the lexicon of the gun, which Al Rindler knew
so well, the edge was on the side of the man who could
put the pressure of the unexpected and of dread
decision on the other fellow. It was an edge that could
speed up the former's moves while slowing those made

in return. Starkly put, it could be the measure of life, or death. No one understood this better than did Rindler himself. It was here now and he recognized it and became hesitant.

The tawny glance he fixed on Cleve Ellerson carried an almost terrible intensity, and tension gathered in him until it was like a taut spring. But the big decision just would not come, choked back by that hesitancy that grew and grew. It was a thing Ellerson had seen in other Al Rindlers he'd met with in the past, and, recognizing it now, his lip curled tauntingly.

'Don't like it this way, eh Rindler? Odds not quite to your liking? Or because it's not the sure thing it was against a clumsy-fisted miner like Ned Tomlin? In which case ...!'

His hand flicked under his coat, came out filled with the weighty bulk of the big .45 Colt gun. He dropped the muzzle of the weapon level, while his words rang with a crisp authority.

'Ackerman, put your hands flat on the table! Rindler, take that shoulder gun of yours and chuck it into yonder corner. Careful how you do it – oh, very, *very* careful! One phony move and ... !' He waggled the Colt meaningly. 'Get at it – both of you.'

They complied with a stilted, frozen care. Hands spread as ordered, Duke Ackerman leaned forward, his flat stare malignant and reptilian. With thumb and forefinger gripping the butt, Al Rindler lifted free his shoulder gun and tossed it aside.

'Exactly right,' Ellerson approved. 'Now I leave without risking a shot in the back.'

Speaking, he reached with his free hand, jerked wide the door and wheeled through, slamming the door shut behind him before driving solidly into Tug Morley who had been hovering close to the door trying to pick up what had been going on in the back room. Ellerson did not hesitate making his next move. He laid the solid weight of his gun across Morley's head and the Lucky Lode bouncer went down in a heap.

Both the house gambler, Carmody, and the bartender, Riordan, watched with fixed, startled care, but neither made any move toward interfering. Wielding a towel, Riordan scrubbed the top of the bar in great, wide sweeps. Carmody was a statue, attentive and still. Moving on toward the street, Ellerson laid out a final word.

'When he's able to listen again, tell Morley that was just part payment for what he did to old Lafe Kenna ...!'

Once outside, Ellerson headed directly back to the freight yard. He was fully aware that he'd just crossed a river of no return, yet felt the better for it. Where Duke Ackerman and company were concerned, he had declared himself, planted his flag beyond any misunderstanding or recall, and the weight of any further indecision was completely off his shoulders. He felt eager and strong and free. That was it – free!

Back in the rear room of the Lucky Lode, tension was like short-fused dynamite. Half crouched in his chair, heavy shoulders hunched forward, Duke Ackerman stared at the closed door with black and bitter anger. Beside him, Al Rindler was a man frozen to immobility by the tumult of wild feeling that convulsed him. At the corners of his nostrils white cavities of repressed passion quivered and his lips formed a pinched and bloodless line. All normal light in his tawny eyes was blotted out by a crimson glare. The atmosphere of the room was thick with baffled frustration.

When Rindler finally moved to recover his gun it was in a stiff, mechanical manner. He looked the weapon over carefully before sliding it back into the holster.

Then his head came up and he whirled on Ackerman as though about to deliver a blow of some kind.

'Go ahead – say it!' he droned wickedly. 'Say it now – say it once – and then never mention it again. Say that Ellerson called me, and that I backed down. Because he did, and I backed down. Don't ask me why – but I did. I backed down. He's not that good, not that much better or faster. No man alive is, yet – I backed down. He called me and I backed down …!'

Over and over he said it, as though repeating a litany of some sort. Slow and strained and unbelieving at first, then faster and faster in a down-sliding, diminishing whisper until the only way Ackerman could tell that he was repeating himself was by the way his lips kept shaping and moving. He was, Ackerman thought, like some sort of fanatical penitent, scourging himself with a whip of scorn, so deep was the wound to his confidence and conceit.

'He called me – and I backed down …!'

As though the words, if repeated often enough, would somehow ease the tumult of feeling that punished him.

On the verge of a jeering remark in an effort to be rid of some of his own frustration, Duke Ackerman held back the scoffing words, fully realizing that at this moment Al Rindler was as dangerous and unpredictable as a coiled rattlesnake. Anything – one careless word or move could loose that seething deadliness. This was clearly a time to speak softly, and Ackerman did so. Also carefully.

'Forget it, Al. You played it smart. He laid it on the line to me, didn't he – laid it on – plenty! and I took it because I know how this gun business goes. We'd been foolish to let him push us into a bad move when he was set for it and we weren't. Hell – there's always another time coming up when the break can be the other way around. *Then* we'll take care of that fellow!'

Staring at the closed door, Rindler did not answer, remaining tight-lipped and quiet, imprisoned in the dark venom of his punishing thoughts.

Came a diffident knock at the door which Ackerman answered harshly. 'All right – what do you want?'

The door eased open and Riordan the bartender peered in cautiously. 'Just wanted to know if everything was all right with you people. Out here, something happened.'

Looking past the hesitant speaker, Duke Ackerman glimpsed a figure sprawled on the barroom floor. Cursing, he surged to his feet.

'Who is that? What the hell happened?'

'Tug Morley,' the bartender explained. 'He ain't dead, just out cold. When that feller Ellerson come bustin' out that door, Tug got in his way and Ellerson buffaloed him – plenty! Tug, he hit the floor and he ain't moved since.'

'Why would Ellerson gunwhip him?' Ackerman demanded.

The bartender shrugged. 'Said it was part payment for somethin' Tug did to that old souse, Lafe Kenna.'

'And what did Morley do to Kenna?'

Riordan shrugged again. 'Cuffed him around some, I think. For trying to cadge drinks. Mebbe Tug did more than that, but I wouldn't know for sure.'

Ackerman moved out into the barroom for a closer look at Morley, who just now began to stir a little. As though finding the bald facts hard to believe, Ackerman reviewed them to himself in a half smothered tone.

'He walks in, reads me off, calls Al Rindler, then buffaloes another of my men on the way out. Just like *that* he does it!'

Voice rising, Ackerman came around sharply on his bartender. 'Why didn't you do something about it, Riordan?'

Riordan started. 'Me? Mix it tough with a feller like that Ellerson? Oh no, Mr Ackerman – not me! I'll pour whiskey across your bar all day and all night should you want it so. But that's where I belong, behind that bar. And that's where I stay!'

Tug Morley groaned and rolled over. He was slack-jawed and all his heavy features were loose and flaccid. Oozing from his dented scalp, blood slanted a crimson line across his forehead. He looked stupid and deflated and uncouth. Ackerman turned away in disgust.

'Pour some water on him.'

Well past midmorning, Lafe Kenna roused and, manipulating board-stiff muscles carefully, left the bunk that had comforted him, located his clothes and dressed. A cold water wash comforted his mauled features somewhat, getting one eye fully opened and loosening the dark bruise about the other until it too gained partial use. With new-found purpose he made up the bunk, then let himself out of the rear door of Scotty Duncan's quarters and peered around the compound. Yonder, just leaving the blacksmith shop, was the tall figure of the man he wanted to see, and he shuffled over there.

'No need you rolling out yet, Lafe,' Cleve Ellerson told him. 'I figured the bunk would hold you for the rest of the day.'

'Not so,' retorted Kenna gruffly. 'I'm still kinda puny all right – but not that damn puny. It was a case of get up now, or never get up. Of stand up now, or never stand up. Never again do I whine or crawl in front of any damn man. Nobody has cause to call me a dog any more. I've cadged my last drink. From here on out, when and if I take a drink, it'll be likker I pay for with my own money, right now I'm lookin' for work – for a job. You know where I can find one?'

Ellerson surveyed the old fellow gravely, saying nothing. Kenna swung an angry shoulder.

'Know what you're thinkin' – and you're wrong. I'm not makin' talk that don't mean anything. Could be Tug Morley did me a favor by clubbin' hell out of me. Could be he gave me the first real look at myself since the devil knows when. And I don't like what I see – not one damn little bit I don't. So I'm changin' things. How about it – do I get a job?'

There was no mistaking the spark of purpose gleaming in Kenna's good eye and past the narrowed slit of the other. He means it, Ellerson marvelled – the old son-of-a-gun really means it ...!

'That would be up to Scotty, Lafe. What do you figure to do?'

'Anything I'm asked to. In my time I've skinned freight outfits with some of the best in the business. I know mules backwards and forwards. I can curry and tend livestock. I can mend a wire cut or heal up a harness sore. I can cold-shoe a critter if I have to. I can grease a wagon. I can soap and mend harness. I can clean feed sheds and stables. Hell man, I can do anything! You name the chore and I'll do it. All I want is the chance to prove I'm a man, standin' on my own two feet – not a dog to be kicked around.'

'Fair enough,' Ellerson told him. 'We'll see what Scotty has to say when he gets in from Chinese Flat later on. In case he says yes and puts you to work, you got to have something besides whiskey in you.' He thumbed a dollar from a pocket and held it out.

'It's coming on noon. Go buy yourself a square meal.'

Eyeing the dollar, Kenna shook his head. 'Obliged, but I ain't takin' nothin' until I earn it.'

'Man, you've got to eat,' Ellerson insisted. 'Call this a loan against your first wages.'

Kenna hesitated, then nodded. 'All right, long as that's the way it is. Just a loan. You'll get it back.'

Shuffling along with a string-halted limp, Lafe Kenna headed uptown, and in spite of his all-over physical misery, carried his thin shoulders erect and his head high. Watching him, Ellerson smiled over his thoughts.

'I got it back already, Lafe. If it buys you a couple of hours of self-respect, it's worth it.'

Lafe Kenna was supremely conscious of that lone silver dollar. In the Lucky Lode it would buy him four whiskies and access to the free lunch shelf. But no sooner did this sly and betraying possibility flash through his mind than it was thrown aside with a short, clench-fisted punch, chopped at empty air.

'None of that, Kenna – none of that!' he objured himself savagely. 'Stand up straight, God damn you! From here on out, you're a man!'

He turned in at the Oliver eating house and as it was still half an hour shy of midday, there was plenty of room at the counter. Just about as pretty a girl as he'd ever seen, smiled at him as she put a meal before him, and that smile took him far back across the years to another pretty girl who once had smiled at him when he was young and the world was fair and wide and full of promise.

It all shaped up as a fine interval in a life that had been a dismal, cheerless mockery. In here it was bright and warm and cheerful, the air savory with good food fragrances. And there was that red-cheeked, clear-eyed girl to smile her kindliness at him. Who had been that other girl in the far, dim past? The one about whom a dream had been wrapped, a dream that never became anything more than that. What had been her name? He shook his head, unable to remember. The picture he was trying to recall just would not take solid shape. It had all been so long, long ago ...

A full hour before the evening shadow flowed down from the hills, Scotty Duncan came in on one of his big freight outfits. He tossed a battered gripsack to Cleve Ellerson and came spryly down off the high box of the Merivale wagon, exclaiming wryly.

'Thank God that's over! Damn slow travel – damn rough, too. Still on the job, I see.'

Ellerson grinned slightly. 'No place else to go. How are things at Chinese Flat?'

'Quiet, and good enough. Anything happen here?'

'Some,' said Ellerson, sobering. 'You're minus a former yard boss. And a miner named O'Dea was knifed.'

'The hell! Knifed? You mean – killed?'

Ellerson nodded. 'Last night. Camp's pretty mad over it, but like Sash Jeffers said, not mad enough to do anything more than smash up Duke Ackerman's sluice boxes.'

Headed for quarters, Scotty stamped angry boot heels. 'Figure Ackerman behind it, eh? Well, more than likely. Damned human lice,' he stormed. 'Ackerman and his crowd – that's all they are, just damn lice – murdering men like O'Dea. I knew Johnny O'Dea. One of the best, and not afraid to stand up for his rights and speak his mind. Which is why they killed him, of course. Robbed him of a good claim, then killed him when he tried to do something about getting it back. Some people in this camp deserve to be hung. Maybe they will be! Now, what's this about my former yard boss – meaning Buck Devlin. What about him?'

'Didn't like me taking over in his place,' Ellerson explained. 'So he began pushing and shoving for a chance to prove he was the better man. Didn't work out like he figured.'

'Doesn't surprise me,' Scotty said. 'Fact is, I expected something of the sort. You had to work him over?'

'Some. Then fired him. Since then, Sash Jeffers saw him acting cozy with Jack Pelly.'

'Now that doesn't surprise me too much, either,' declared Scotty, succinctly blunt. 'One of the reasons I intended to get rid of him. I've wondered why the stage holdup occurred on that particular trip when there was the heavy gold shipment aboard. Maybe this explains it.'

'Sash Jeffers told me about that,' Ellerson said, 'and it figures. So tomorrow morning I ride out to where it happened. I'll pick up trail sign and I'll follow it. Be interesting to see where it leads.'

Stepping into his quarters, Scotty exclaimed his satisfaction. 'Good to be back. Man's like an old dog – never real comfortable away from his own kennel. Didn't sleep worth a damn in Chinese Flat last night. Missed my own bunk.'

'Somebody else made use of your bunk last night,' Ellerson told him.

Scotty stared. 'So?'

Briefly, Ellerson sketched the affair with Lafe Kenna. 'Tough old cuss though,' he added. 'Up and around again now, ready to spit in the eye of the world. Vows he's through being a bum and is looking for a job.'

Scotty's small smile was cynical. 'I've seen drunks swear off before. The good intentions last only until the big thirst hits again.'

'Does run that way,' Ellerson admitted. 'But once in a while it's for real. Maybe old Lafe deserves a chance to prove it.'

Scotty frowned. 'But what can he do?'

Ellerson grinned. 'He claims anything you want to name. Any and every kind of chore that comes up around a compound like this. Kind of sold me. I staked him to a dollar for a square meal. He wouldn't take it unless strictly as a loan to be paid back first time he draws wages.'

Scotty's glance was quiet and shrewdly measuring. This man Ellerson was sure something apart from the usual run. In some ways as tough as they came, but at the same time owning a broad streak of real kindness. And he's really pulling for old Lafe, realized Scotty. With this conclusion, he made up his mind.

'Guess I'll have to give Kenna a try to make sure you get your dollar back. Tomorrow, find something for him to do.' The matter settled, Scotty became sober and concerned again. 'Sure stirs me up about Johnny O'Dea. As I said – such a good man. He had a sizable poke of gold going out on the stage that was robbed. I'll have to trace down his kin and make it good to them. I say it again – damn all the thieves and rotten killers,' he ended fiercely.

'Just so,' affirmed Ellerson. 'Had me a little talk with Duke Ackerman on that point.'

Scotty exclaimed. 'Where did you see Ackerman?'

'His private hide-out, back room of the Lucky Lode. This morning. Told him if anything more happened against our layout that shouldn't, I'd call on him personal! Told him the same went for him or any others of his crowd where Jim Oliver and his women folks were concerned. I think he got the idea.'

Again Scotty exclaimed. 'Be damned! Man, you amaze me. Called him right in his own burrow, eh? Long chance – long chance! Wasn't that pet gunny of his, Al Rindler around?'

'On hand and itching to start something,' Ellerson said. 'I invited him to go ahead and make his try if he thought he could get there. He didn't want any, not right at that moment. But I'll have to watch that fellow.'

Scotty studied him again, as though hardly able to believe his ears. Then, with sudden impulse, he slapped Ellerson on the shoulder. 'The day you came into this camp, my luck sure changed.'

At the first edge of a powder-blue dusk, Jack Pelly emerged from his cabin. He had looked at the bottom of his bottle, then slept the afternoon away. Cold water, liberally applied, inside and out, had washed away the worst of the dregs of a mild hangover and now he was hungry and thinking of the free lunch shelf in the Lucky Lode. He entered the place with the first of the early crowd, found a place at the bar and looked around.

On the face of it, all appeared as usual. The houseman gambler, Carmody, had a stud game going at his favorite poker table and play had already started at the faro layout, with Al Rindler tight-jawed and intent on the lookout stool. The only disturbing note was Tug Morley and his appearance. Instead of patrolling the room in his usual way, Morley was now holding down a chair in a far inner corner, a makeshift bandage around his dented head. His expression was loose and surly and stupid. Pelly looked across his shoulder at the bartender.

'What the hell happened to Morley, Pat?'

Riordan kept his answer low and confidential. 'That new feller in camp – that Ellerson – he buffaloed Tug, parted his hair with the barrel of a forty-five. Never saw a neater, quicker job of it. Tug went down and out and never moved until considerable later. Boss made me throw some water on him to bring him round. Ackerman was sure scalded, hisself.

'Now this is hard to believe, Jack – but it happened, sure enough. That feller Ellerson come into here, actin' like he knew exactly where he was goin', and what for. He barged right on into the back room, without knockin' or by your leave or anything of the sort. Just pushed right in, told off the boss and called Al Rindler – cold!

'Rindler backed down. Yessir, that's what he did, Jack – he backed down! And now that fact is eatin' him alive. He's strung so tight over it you can smell the poison in him, just like you can smell a mean old rattlesnake that's on the peck. Wouldn't go near him, was I you, or say anything to him about it right now. And you know, Jack – for the first time since I been here, I'm feeling' a little shaky about things. I'm tellin' you that when that feller Ellerson walked through here after doin' all he did to me he looked ten feet tall. Yes, sir, Jack, things are sure changin' in this camp. What do you think?'

'As I see it, you're more than half right,' Pelly said. 'All along I've felt it only needed one good man to start real trouble and shake things apart for us. And it strikes me that in Ellerson, Scotty Duncan found that man. I been trying to tell it so to Duke Ackerman, but he won't listen; he's so far gone with gold fever he can't see six inches past the end of his nose in some ways. Well, I'm riding out to the cabin tomorrow and Smiley Slade's sure to be wanting a bottle. I'll want one, too, for my cabin. And you can pour me a regular shot to go with my supper.'

Pelly carried his drink over to the free lunch shelf, had his supper there. Afterwards he picked up his bottles and headed back to his cabin under a blue-black sky from which the stars peered dimly through a high, cold haze. In the solitary stillness of his cabin, after tapping his bottle a couple of times, he stretched out in his blankets, threshed out dark thoughts and made dark plans.

EIGHT

Riding the creek flats, Jack Pelly tested the mood of the miners by dropping a casual nod here and there. Most showed him little response and no friendliness at all. One reaction was unmistakable. A gray-beard crouched at the creek's edge over a gold pan returned a hard, unwinking stare. After which he spat tobacco juice in Pelly's direction with an emphasis not to be misread. Here was the extreme of a scathing contempt and it stirred such dark anger in Pelly his impulse was to get down and boot the man bodily into the creek. But the sly and basic caution so much a part of him, kept him in the saddle.

The further he rode the less interested he was in putting out a show of authority. It was only an empty front at best, with no real meaning. Also, solidly in his mind was the conviction that Duke Ackerman and all his works were about done in this camp. In which case, where did that leave him? Not, if he could help it, dangling from a rope as did the two wild ones in that well-rememberd former camp.

Still and all, Ackerman would expect a report of some kind and was shrewd enough to tell the difference between a semblance of the real thing and something made up of whole cloth. And, it was important to get some idea of what was definitely known and what was merely suspected in the knife murder of Johnny O'Dea. So now he sought the spot of the crime.

In front of the rude brush and canvas shanty that had been O'Dea's living quarters, half a dozen miners were gathered, sorting out some scanty belongings. Here, Pelly immediately sensed the usual harsh mood of distrust, and they were ominously silent as he rode up and dismounted. He indicated the pitiful pile of personal effects.

'What about these?'

There was no immediate answer. Finally one of the group gave a reluctant shrug.

'Johnny O'Dea's gear. Me, I'm Toby Stent, I was Johnny's nearest neighbor, and the one who found his body. We aim to sell this gear and send the money to Johnny's kin, if we can locate any. Maybe you might know something about that?'

Pelly shook his head. 'Not off hand. I did hear he had some dust going out on the stage that was held up. In which case Scotty Duncan should have some word about where it was being sent. You could ask him about that.'

'Makes sense,' admitted Toby Stent. 'We'll try it.'

Pelly seized on the opening. 'You were the one who found O'Dea? Let's have the story.'

Typical of his kind, Toby Stent was gnarled by hard work, methodical and slow speaking. He frowned a careful way along.

'My coffee pot sprung a leak. I knew Johnny had a spare so I borrowed it. When I brought it back, Johnny's fire was burned down and Johnny was lying there. When I spoke, he didn't answer. I took a closer look. He was dead, knifed in the back. That's all I know, except that I spread the word. Me, I'm a peaceable man, but right now I'd sure enjoy helping hang the low-down scut who killed Johnny!'

He ended with a flare of defiance that won a growl of approval from the others in the group. 'Plenty of us would pull on that rope,' one of them said.

Jack Pelly shook a reproving head. 'Can't have that, boys. Know how you feel, but a thing of this sort has to be handled through the law, not by a lynch mob.' He ran his glance over the group before bringing it back to Toby Stent.

'You never saw anybody prowling around? Or heard anything like a call or cry from O'Dea?'

'Nothing,' Toby Stent said. 'It was thick early dark about then and I never heard or saw a thing out of the way until I found Johnny lying dead right here.'

Again Pelly shook his head, making the gesture as rueful and regretful as he could. 'A mean deal all around. Now I got to try and run down the killer with no solid place to start from, and be blamed if I don't come up with the right answer out of all this thousand miles of wild country. Did I say it was mean …?'

He got no answer, just an ominous silence that closed him out and made it plain there was no place for him in this group. He climbed back into his saddle, looked down and tapped the badge on his shirt.

'Anybody thinks packing this is an easy chore can have my job whenever they want it.'

He rode on, then, down the full run of the open flats and into the timber beyond, crossing the creek at a rushing shallows where his horse snatched a drink while splashing through. Once in the safe covert of the timber he pulled up to build a smoke and have a long and careful look at his back trail.

The unease in him was growing steadily. He had shown his best front to that group back there and it had done no good. He had met a hard, unyielding wall of animosity and distrust; silent, yet purposeful. And the feeling was on him that what he had met back there was following him. Something without visible substance, a shadow so thin you couldn't see it. Yet – definitely something ...!

He pushed ahead into the timber, slanting off at an angle to strike a dim trail of hoof marks that took him steadily deeper into the hill country, looping through a series of minor ups and downs before facing a loftier crest, then topping this and dropping on into a basin of big timber beyond.

This was wild, remote country, far off the regular paths of men. Pelly, however, knew where he was going and presently moved out of the timber into a narrow, climbing meadow. At the upper end of the meadow crouched a low, sod-roofed, deeply weathered cabin and beyond the cabin a split rail corral held a sorrel horse. At Pelly's approach a burly, thick-shouldered man with short, bowed legs stepped into sight, a rifle against the cabin wall. Reining up, Jack Pelly made mild observation.

'Spooky this morning, Smiley?'

'Some – and with reason,' was the guttural-toned reply. 'Had a damn close call the other night, close enough to last me for some time. Duke Ackerman wants any more jobs pulled like that one, he can do it himself. Hardly had my man down and done for than one of his neighbors came blundering along. I barely got clear. It wasn't easy.'

'I can understand that,' Pelly agreed. 'But you better hope Ackerman understands, too. He wants to see you tonight and he's real worked up because you didn't hide the body.'

'Hide – hell!' was the harsh, explosive reply. 'Had all I could do to hide myself. Strikes me Ackerman is beginnin' to want too damn much for too damn little. If those miners had nailed me, it would have been Smiley Slade's hide hung up to dry, not Duke Ackerman's. But you're just in time. Coffee's turnin' over. Light down. By chance would you have a bottle with you?'

Pelly produced one from a saddle bag. 'My friend, you're in luck.'

'Luck is what I need,' grunted Slade, clutching the bottle greedily and leading the way into the cabin. It was a single small room, made even more cramped by the pile of riding and traveling gear stacked in the middle of it. Barely enough space was left for a blanketed wall bunk, a rusty sheepherder stove, a small board table and two short benches. Roving the place, Pelly's glance turned sober.

'See you're still hanging on to that pack saddle Ackerman told you to get rid of. He knew it was still here he'd be liable to turn Al Rindler loose on you.'

Bolstered by a heavy jolt of whiskey, Smiley Slade leered. 'What Ackerman don't know won't hurt him. What's worrying him?'

'Wouldn't want to risk somebody seeing it, recognizing it and start wondering about Danny Yokum.'

Smiley Slade's scoffing laugh was rough and harsh. 'What the hell! Nobody ever comes by here. Lonesomest damn hole I ever was in. Man could go loco hangin' around here too long. Far as Danny Yokum is concerned, you know where we planted him. He's still there. That pack saddle is too good a one to destroy just because it's got some initials burned on it. And when it comes time for Smiley Slade to haul out of this country, that pack saddle will be toting his gear.'

Pelly's soberness deepened. 'Hauling out of these parts is what I want to talk about with you, Smiley. And I'm saying the time to go is – *now!* The camp is edgy and getting worse all the time. I've tried to make Ackerman see that. But he won't, being too completely gold crazy to see past the end of his nose. He claims the camp will quiet down again. Even with his sluice boxes smashed up he's talking about rebuilding them. Which would sure be baiting the bear! Now me, I can see where a man could want a pretty sizeable stake, but not at the price of a lynch rope around his neck.'

Smiley Slade studied him with little, lead-colored eyes. 'That angle worries you a lot, doesn't it! You've mentioned it before. What you so afraid of?'

'You ever see a man die on the end of a rope, Smiley? Well I have – I saw two of them go like that. And I can think of a lot better ways.'

'Bad as that, eh?' Slade grunted. 'You really think a necktie party could be shaping up?'

'I'd bet on it. And I'm remembering a miners' court that operated at the Midas Hill diggings; how fast it worked and how sure it worked. When it was done, there were two gay lads kicking on air. And when a man starts toting up his chances of ending that way, well – what do *you* think?'

Smiley Slade filled a tin cup with coffee and pushed it across the table, speaking slowly.

'I've always figured a man had just so much luck. And when he gets the feeling that his luck is about to run out, then it's time to move on. The other night, my luck ran awful thin, so you could be right – it's time to travel. But not with empty pockets. It's high time Ackerman came across with our full share. And he never has let on how much you and me took off that stage.'

'Not to me. But I heard Scotty Duncan claims right on six thousand dollars' worth.'

Smiley Slade's murky eyes took on a gleam. 'According to that deal, it was to be a three-way split.

Which works out at a couple of thousand for each of us. Now I figure a man could live free and easy for a considerable time on that kind of money. Besides that, for other jobs we've done, there should be considerable more coming our way. So maybe you and me, we should brace Mister Duke Ackerman for our shares. And the quicker the sooner – like tonight. How about it?'

'You're talking my language, Smiley,' said Pelly swiftly. 'Tonight it is – at the Lucky Lode. I'll be waiting for you. And,' he added warningly, 'it's quite possible Ackerman may try to hedge the bet. From this and that he's said at times, I've had to wonder. And if he does try to short-change us, he'll have Al Rindler to back his hand.'

Smiley Slade's leaden eyes turned murky and the thrust of his heavy jaw made his face brute heavy and ugly. 'You really think he'd try to hedge on us?'

'Call it an even chance. I told you he was gold crazy.'

'He better not try it on me!' The guttural note in Slade's voice deepened. 'Nobody ever cheated me out of a dollar and made it stick. Feller tried it one time on a cattle ranch where I rode. Took me down to my last dime in a stud poker game with the craziest run of luck I ever met up with. More I thought about it the more it came to me that nobody could have such a run of luck without buggerin' the cards somehow. So I waited my chance – with this.' He slid a hand inside his shirt and came up with a long, heavy-bladed Bowie knife. 'Had to use it on him to keep him quiet. But I got my money back, and then some!'

Jack Pelly looked at the glittering blade, then as quickly looked away. That had to be the knife that had let the life out of Johnny O'Dea not too many hours ago. Pelly covered the moment of his small panic and squeamishness with a gulp of coffee.

'God damn a knife!' he thought. 'And the same for a man who'll use one. A bullet is clean. But a knife … ! this fellow Slade is all animal. I'll use him as long as I need him, but once I'm clear of him and Ackerman and Rindler, I stay clear for good.' He returned his cup to the table and made ready to leave. 'Tonight it is, Smiley. At the Lucky Lode.'

'I'll be there,' Slade promised. 'I'll bring the other horses down from the upper pasture where I've been keeping them. Good strong talking point, those horses, should Ackerman turn stubborn about our share of the haul. Because, come need of that quick getaway he used to mention, he'd be in a hell of a fix without horses to put his ridin' gear on.'

Selecting a saddle from the cabin's clutter, Slade lugged it and his rifle around and cinched the saddle on the corral's lone occupant. Thereupon he rode away into the timber at the clearing's upper end. Heading the opposite way, Jack Pelly followed the run of a small brush-shrouded water course that would, after several twisting miles, empty its meager contents into the hurrying flow of Rawhide Creek, just below town.

At the same time Jack Pelly met with the miners at Johnny O'Dea's camp, Cleve Ellerson left the creek flats by way of the main road. The horse he rode was a good one, a short coupled roan that was eager and strong enough to take the lift of the grade at a steady, reaching trot.

How long, he mused, since he'd last known the moulded comfort of saddle leather and the lift of spirited horseflesh under him? Much too long, he decided, and in good time he'd get back to it again, for a man born and raised to the saddle belonged there and nowhere else. These were the kind of thoughts to revive memories of many things.

Like, for instance, a picture of that string of spring-fed meadows back on the Garrison Hills range, where he had once ridden. There a man could build himself a cabin, make a start with a few head of white-faced cattle and by hard work and a little luck, build himself into a solid citizen, with the old, wild days left behind forever.

Pleasant enough fancies all right, but Ellerson shook himself free of them. Time enough for such in a more settled future, should that future ever arrive. Right now, what lay ahead was unpredictable and full of grim possibilities. To remind him of this was the rifle slung under his stirrup leather. He'd been about to leave when Scotty Duncan came over with the Winchester and a pair of saddle bags.

'Yeah, I know,' Scotty grumbled, 'you got a hand gun and you know how to use it. But Pony Bob McCart and Jake Rivers were rifle shot, and should you happen to meet up with the killers, you'll need more than a Colt to stand an even chance. There's fodder for the Winchester in the saddle bags.'

Watching Ellerson strap rifle and saddle bags into place, Scotty had more to say.

'Something for you to remember. This is no one-man, personal crusade, understand. What you're after belongs to me and Jim Oliver to Pete Yost and all the other decent people in this camp. It belongs to the memory of Pony Bob McCart and Jake Rivers, and of Ned Tomlin and Johnny O'Dea. And from what Jim Oliver claims, it goes for the memory of Danny Yokum, too – the man who made the Discovery strike and started the camp. Just the same, should you have to throw lead to stay alive, then throw it! Now get along with you – and good luck!'

The steady drive of the roan soon had Ellerson at the

spot of the stage holdup. He reined in, looking the area over, visualizing things as they had been. Yonder was where the stage and team had stood. Here had lain one dead man and over there lay the second. Just now it was all an empty world save for the restless churning of swarms of green flies, buzzing about the spots where good men had died and darkened the clotted earth with their blood.

Ellerson reined the roan around and circled to the spot behind the jackpine thicket which he had located the day of the holdup. Here, plainly enough, horses had been tied, and in their restlessness had scuffed and trampled the earth. As Ellerson read things, two horses had been here, and though the sign was now old enough to smudge out in some places, deep hoof gouges in the soft forest duff leading away from the spot were enough to point a sure direction. When Ellerson put the roan to it the trail became a down-hill slant which took him around the lower end of the creek flats. Here it crossed the creek itself and drove away through deep timber toward the higher hill country beyond.

Well into the timber, traveling with a steady, willing purpose, the roan suddenly lifted an alert, ear-pricked head and snorted softly. Lifting high in his saddle, Ellerson serched for the cause of this and found it in another set of hoof prints angling in from the side. These were freshly cut, only minutes old. But on all sides the timber aisles now were still and empty. Ellerson sent the roan ahead at a more contained pace.

The trail, old sign and new, wound and climbed through a considerable stretch of rough country before finally angling up the flank of a fairly lofty ridge. Cresting this, Ellerson met a drift of air pungent with the scent of wood smoke and he hauled up to test this and its source. The fact that smoke lifted as well as drifted, placed that source somewhere in the timber basin beyond the ridge.

He worked a careful way along the ridge crest until, presently, through a gap in the timber he looked down at a clearing which held a small, weatherbeaten cabin and a split rail corral. A sorrel horse stood hip-shot in the corral and another horse, a bay, under saddle, was ground reined at the cabin door. The stumpy, rusty chimney of the cabin gave off a thin winnowing of smoke.

Ellerson tied the roan back in deeper cover, fed a handful of cartridges through the loading gate of the Winchester, jacked a load into the chamber and returned to where he could watch the cabin. Here the world was still, so quiet that when a pair of Douglas squirrels struck up a small, barking quarrel, the sound was startling.

That saddle horse, Ellerson decided, would be the one that made the fresh sign along the trail. He could only guess at who it had carried, and what the rider was doing here. For this he soon had part of the answer. Two men emerged from the cabin, one shouldering a saddle. The taller of the two, now about to swing up on the bay horse, was Jack Pelly. The other, the one with the saddle, was a figure out of the lately recalled past. There was no mistaking that figure – short, wide almost simian. Ellerson exclaimed softly, framing the name.

'Smiley Slade! And the same!'

Here was the cabin and the man Lafe Kenna had told of. Here also, the end of a trail that led directly from the scene of the holdup. Sign showed that two men pulled that trick and killed driver and guard. And here were two men who surely knew that trail – and had made it!

While Ellerson watched, Slade quick-circled to the corral, caught and saddled the sorrel, then rode away into the timber at the far end of the clearing while Jack Pelly rode the other way and out the lower end.

Soberly, Ellerson weighed his next move. If he returned to Scotty Duncan with only what he now knew, while it surely meant something, it could also be only guesswork and conjecture. What was needed was some sort of solid proof. Which meant a look in that cabin, to see what it held. The place seemed empty. There was no further sign of life around save that thin haze of smoke drifting from the chimney. If anyone was still in the cabin and caught him approaching in the open, he'd be a sitting duck. Nor could he risk too much time in making up his mind.

Even as he pondered the problem the smoke from the chimney thinned to a mere wisp, then faded altogether. The fire had gone out, to suggest that the cabin was really empty. The thought fathered the action. Rifle half raised, ready for instant use, Ellerson went down the slope with long, plunging strides, struck the flat and crossed swiftly to the cabin. His gamble was good. The place was empty save for a variety of stale human and animal odors and he made swift survey of it and what it held.

Even smaller than it had appeared from the outside, most of it was taken up with a tangle of riding equipment. Some half dozen stock saddles were piled together and a lone sawbuck pack saddle lay in a corner by itself. A tangled heap held bridles, hackamores, saddle bags. Three scabbarded rifles were laid against a wall. Left was only bare living, eating and sleeping space for one person. Yet, here was riding equipment for several.

Spurred by the significance of it, Ellerson wondered about that lone pack saddle and he picked it up for closer examination. Burned into the wood of one fork were two letters. *D.Y.* they were obviously initials, set there to prove ownership. Ellerson waited for nothing more. He replaced the pack saddle as he had found it, moved to the cabin door for a careful look around, saw a still quiet world and climbed quickly back to where he had left the roan. In saddle, he cut down around the clearing's lower end and picked up Jack Pelly's trail of departure. He followed this at an easy pace and was in no way surprised when it led him into the Rawhide Creek flats not far from town.

At the compound he found Lafe Kenna waiting, to brace him before he could get out of the saddle. 'Well,' demanded the old fellow, 'do I, or don't I?'

Ellerson grinned. 'Ready to go, eh – all bright-eyed and bushy-tailed? Fair enough. You can start by taking care of this horse. And it's a good one.'

Kenna reached for the reins, exclaiming, 'Man – just watch me!'

Ellerson found Scotty Duncan at his desk. Scotty showed some surprise.

'Quick trip. Means you either found nothing or something. Which is it?'

'Something,' Ellerson said. 'You and me should go see Jim Oliver. He'll be interested.'

Scotty pushed his paper work aside, got his hat and pipe and led out the door, grumbling good naturedly. 'Sounds important.'

'I'll let you and Oliver judge,' Ellerson said.

At the eating house, Holly Yarnell faced them. 'If you're looking for food, you're too early.'

'No food, youngster,' rumbled Scotty. 'Just a talk with Jim Oliver.'

She led them back to the cozy living room where Jim Oliver held down one of the rocking chairs. He waved Scotty to the other. Ellerson hunkered down against a wall and got out his tobacco and papers. While he was twisting up a smoke, Scotty explained the visit.

'Ellerson here borrowed a horse from me and took a ride this morning, Jim. He says he has something to tell us.'

Ellerson made it brief, telling of what he'd found at the scene of the holdup, of the trail he'd followed and where it led him. He told of the cabin and the two men he saw there and what he'd found inside the cabin. When he told of the pack saddle, Jim Oliver leaned forward.

'The initials were D.Y.? You're sure?'

'No question,' Ellerson nodded. 'D.Y. they were!'

'Which proves what I've felt all along is true,' Jim Oliver said grimly. 'That was Danny Yokum's pack saddle. Hell, man – I watched him burn those initials one evening at the Granite Lake diggings. We were sitting around the stove listening to Danny tell of some of his wanderings. Helen had discarded an old kitchen fork with a broken tine. Danny heated it in the stove and used it to burn his initials. It means of course that Danny is dead, that Duke Ackerman killed him personally, or had him killed, so he could grab off the Discovery claim. Either way, Ackerman is guilty as hell!'

'Just so,' Scotty growled. 'And Jack Pelly was one of the two men at the cabin? What a rotten fake that fellow is! The other one – you called him Slade – you knew of him somewhere else?'

Ellerson nodded again. 'That's right. During the Tarpe Grant range war he rode for the same outfit I did. Overnight he disappeared, after knifing an old wrangler to death and robbing him of money won in a poker game.'

'Knife man, eh? Well, here's Jim who was cut. And Johnny O'Dea killed. This Slade did it, you think?'

'It figures,' Ellerson said.

'Also,' went on Scotty, 'him and Pelly could have pulled the stage holdup. In which case, they're both bloody handed scoundrels, with Ackerman standing behind them. Jim, we've plenty here to interest a miners' court.'

'Would seem so,' Oliver agreed. 'But right now I can't do a thing – can't even leave the house. It'll take another week at least before I'll be any use.'

'I'll round the men up,' Scotty vowed. 'I'll do the talking.'

Ellerson wagged a dissenting head. 'Won't do either way. Any night and overnight, Ackerman and his crowd could pull out. Their riding gear is in that cabin and there are horses out there somewhere, according to what Lafe Kenna told me. Also, while some of the miners are mad, not enough of them are. You'll get nowhere there, Scotty. This thing has to be handled different.'

'And how would that be?' Scotty demanded.

'Round them up and lock them up, one at a time. Cut them down to size that way. They're a tough crew, make no mistake there. You try rounding them up in a bunch, some good people could get killed – maybe you. Better leave this to me.'

'*You* – alone?'

'That's right. I understand this kind of business and know what to expect and how to handle it. I bring them in – you lock them up. You got a place that would hold them?'

Scotty began to sputter. 'There's a room in my warehouse that would do. But I can't let you take that kind of a chance.'

'And I,' chimed in Jim Oliver, 'must wonder why you would offer to. You don't owe that much to this camp or to anyone in it. So, why would you?'

Ellerson considered, frowning. 'Suppose we say for

several reasons, all good ones. First, several men have died here because of Duke Ackerman and his crowd. I did not personally know any of them, but from all I can hear they were good men and honest, I did know the one who died under Smiley Slade's knife back on the Tarpe Grant range. That one was Cappy Jenkins. I liked old Cappy, who deserved something better than what he got.' Aware of further question in Jim Oliver's glance, Ellerson answered it bluntly. 'No, I make no pose as being a savior of my fellow man, but I can and do get damned good and mad when decent men are shot off a stage box or knifed in the back. Yeah, I can come up a couple of notches over that sort of mangy business!'

Jim Oliver nodded. 'Understandable. Would there be more?'

'Some. Say I find it necessary to square myself with myself and in the eyes of certain other people. There are some years of general uselessness to be made up for. Seems there comes a time when a man has to stand up and prove his size and worth. For me, that time is now and the place is here. I can't explain it any better than that.'

'All right, you've made it clear,' growled Scotty, getting up to leave. 'But I still say this is miners' court business. So you sit quiet and out of sight while I talk with some of the men. Right, Jim?'

'It should be the business of all the camp,' Oliver agreed.

On the way out, they met Holly Yarnell again. She marked the soberness of their expressions and questioned it.

'Don't tell me there's been more trouble, more people hurt – or killed?'

''Tis not a thing for you to worry your head about,' Scotty told her.

She dropped a hand on Ellerson's arm, looking up at him gravely. 'Cleve, is he telling the truth?'

He marveled at the stir of emotion the mere presence of this gentle girl with the warm cheeks and the quirk of sweetness about her lips brought to him. He smiled down at her.

'We'll do our best to keep out of trouble.'

Her glance followed him as he went out, her brow still pulled in a frown of worry. In spite of his smile and his reassuring words, she had sensed a certain bleakness in him, heightened by the lift of his shoulders and the cast of his head. It was, she thought, the same mood she had sensed in him the day he climbed back to the stage seat beside her after surveying another stage left empty and looted, with two dead men lying in the road.

Out in the street, Scotty paused to repeat himself. 'Remember, you sit tight until I get back. Jim Oliver's right. You don't owe the camp or anybody in it a damn thing. So let the camp take care of its own troubles.'

There was, Ellerson saw, no use arguing the point with this staunchly determined, stubborn Scotsman. 'Fly to it,' he said. 'But don't get your hopes too high. You could find yourself a lone voice, crying in the wilderness. The average miner isn't going to be too interested in going after Duke Ackerman unless he's hurt personally, and bad.'

Scotty's blue eyes glinted. 'Don't be so damned cynical! Lot of good men in this camp.'

Ellerson shrugged. 'Hope you're right.'

They left it that way, Scotty heading up town while Ellerson returned to quarters. Here on a rack with some other guns was the sawed-off Greener shotgun that had been under the hand of Jake Rivers when he lay dead at the scene of the stage holdup. Ellerson hefted the big gun, broke it open and peered through its gaping barrels. At close range, blasting buckshot, it would be a fearsome weapon.

At midday Ellerson returned to the eating house. Holly Yarnell was her usual crisp, industrious self, but it was a busy hour and when she put his dinner before him she had time only for a knowing glance and brief smile. While he ate, Ellerson was alert to the talk around him. Not once did he hear the name of Johnny O'Dea mentioned. But there was much excited concern over the rich streak one Tom McMurtry had struck.

'Heard tell Tom had five straight pans runnin' a good forty dollars each,' one miner declared enthusiastically. 'A man could get rich fast at that rate. Tom'll be celebrating tonight.'

No doubt of that, mused Ellerson sardonically. And Duke Ackerman would get the most of those forty-dollar pans! So of what account was a dead man of a couple of nights ago against the promise of raw yellow gold and plenty of Duke Ackerman's whiskey tonight? Ackerman had these miners figured right. Good enough men in their way, but lambs to the slaughter at the hands of the vicious and the unscrupulous …!

Two hours later, Scotty Duncan returned to his office, tired and disgruntled. Facing Ellerson he glowered in angry disgust.

'You were right,' he confessed harshly. 'They've weakened down already. Johnny O'Dea's dead and buried, ain't he? So what's the good of starting a ruckus now when there's gold waiting to be dug? That's the way it is – that's the way they feel. With them, it's to hell with it! I'm ready to say the same. To hell with it …!'

Ellerson shook his head. 'That's not the answer, either. They held up your stage, didn't they? And took a shot at you? Well, what's to keep them from doing it again?'

Scotty looked at the shotgun on the rack. 'Maybe that Greener gun. I can load that, walk into Ackerman's deadfall and blow his head off. I've a notion to do it, too.'

'You'd never get that far.'

Scotty scrubbed an irritable hand across his face. 'What else can I do?'

'Let me handle it my way.'

'Which,' scowled Scotty, 'would be admitting I'm not up to skinning my own snakes. Besides which, you don't owe ...'

'We've been over all that,' cut in Ellerson bluntly. 'Say I don't owe you anything. I'm concerned with what I owe myself. Now do we do it my way together, or do I do it my way alone?'

Scotty waved a resigned hand. 'All right, have it your own way. I'm supposed to be stubborn. Ain't in it with you! So you bring them in and I'll lock them up. Though I don't know what you'll do about it if they refuse to come.'

Something dark and cold narrowed Ellerson's eyes and built a harshness about his mouth. 'They'll come,' he said quietly. 'One way or another – they'll come ...!'

He moved to the door. 'I'm going to look around.'

As soon as the door closed, Scotty hurried out the back way and accosted a stable hand in the compound.

'Seen Lafe Kenna around?'

The stable hand pointed. 'Harness shed, soapin' gear.'

In the shed's shadowed half-light, Lafe Kenna was busy over a tangle of harness. The air was pungent with the smell of saddle soap. Kenna looked up inquiringly.

'That can wait, Lafe,' Scotty told him. 'I've another job for you. Come along to the office.'

Lafe wiped his hands on a gunny sack and hurried after him. In the office, Scotty faced him.

'Ever handle a revolver, Lafe?'

'In the old days, plenty of times. Was pretty good with one, too. I've seen my share of rough times. Why you askin'?'

'Like this,' said Scotty, making it slow to add emphasis. He outlined what Cleve Ellerson intended to do. 'I'm not saying he ain't man enough to put it across. But no matter how good any man is, he can't do a full job of watching what's behind him all the time. So I want you to watch Ellerson's back. People are used to seeing you along the street, so your being around will seem natural enough. I'm staking you to a Colt gun and I want you to see that nobody sneaks up on Ellerson's blind side. Can I depend on you?'

'Depend on me? Try me – just try me!' The words were husky and fervent with feeling.

Scotty pointed to a holstered gun and cartridge belt hanging from a peg of the rifle rack. 'That's it – take it. It's yours.'

Scotty had never seen greater blaze of purpose show in any man as when Lafe Kenna hefted the gun, then murmured, almost reverently.

'God! It's great to stand straight up again ...!'

NINE

In the Lucky Lode, affairs were fiddle-string taut. Al
Rindler was like a panther, prowling the confines of a
cage. Banked wickedness was a glitter in his tawny eyes
and the pull of tension made a hard-angled mask of his
face. An inner fire was consuming this man, fed
constantly by a scourging knowledge that would not let
him be.

'I backed down ...!'

In the rear room the atmosphere was little better.
Duke Ackerman's ego and confidence were both
suffering; he, too, was plagued by the memory and
bitter facts of Cleve Ellerson's visit. That any man could
have faced him down in this very room, made Al
Rindler take water, then buffalo a lesser hired hand on
the way out – all of which Ellerson had done – though
hard to believe, was indubitably true.

Of it all, Al Rindler's defection was the hardest to
understand and accept. From the first, Rindler and his
ready gun had been a big hole card. He was the one who
would stop trouble in its tracks and put the fear of God
in any doubters; who would guarantee the security of
this room and take full care of any and all physical
threats. He was the trouble-shooter to make the whole
scheme go. Now here was the harsh realization that

perhaps Rindler was not the solid support he was supposed to be. Here could be a weak spot where a weak spot could not be afforded.

All afternoon Duke Ackerman had been reviewing these uncomfortable facts and the nagging suggestions to be drawn from them. Also, all afternoon he'd been trying to drown out his persistent uneasiness. He reached for the bottle to pour still another soothing shot, but found the bottle empty. Mumbling a curse he threw it aside and the clatter of it along the floor came near to covering the knock on the door. Ackerman dropped a hand to the gun in his coat pocket before calling harsh summons.

'All right – all right – come on in!'

It was Jack Pelly, dark-faced and secretive as he pushed through the door. Ackerman relaxed, took his hand from his pocket.

'Time you were showing up. How are things along the flats?'

'Not good,' Pelly told him. 'There's plenty of feeling – and none of it friendly.'

'You get out to the cabin?'

'And saw Smiley. He'll be in tonight.'

'What did he have to say for himself on the O'Dea affair?'

'Did the best he could. One of O'Dea's neighbors came near to walking in on him. Had no chance to get rid of the body. Barely made it clear as it was.'

'Always some damn thing.' Ackerman glowered at the table top. 'Everything handy and ready at the cabin?'

'Seemed so to me.' Pelly's glance sharpened. 'You figuring on moving out?'

Evading direct answer, Ackerman's scowl deepened. 'Depends. Right now I'd like to know what Scotty Duncan and that fellow Ellerson are up to. Maybe you better take a swing around camp and see if you can pick up anything that will give me some idea.'

The old unease was astir in Jack Pelly again. This man owned a sly wariness that could pick up a false note or the slightest change in the feel of things. Right here was such a note to be caught and considered carefully. The room was rank with stale whiskey fumes and there was that empty bottle lying on the floor. Ackerman's face was bloated and heavily flushed and his answers somehow unsure and evasive. Pelly's tone hardened.

'Knew something was out of kilter the minute I came in and saw Rindler. Passing him I slapped him on the shoulder, friendly like. Hell, you'd have thought I shot him. He came around on me fast as a rattlesnake and had that damned gun of his jammed half way through me. And his eyes were tiger wild. What's wrong with him?'

Ackerman relaxed a bare trifle, a sardonic glint in his protuberant eyes. 'Friend Al has had a good look at himself and doesn't like what he saw. That bad man image he's so proud of is all shot to hell. There's a hole in it. When Ellerson called him, right here in this room, Al took water. That Ellerson's a tough one. Wish we had him on our side.'

'Maybe he's the one who will do it,' Pelly offered.

'Do what?'

'Organise the camp against us. Maybe that's what Scotty Duncan hired him for.'

'Thought of that,' admitted Ackerman with a show of irritation. 'But there's no real reason for us to cut and run just yet. It's too easy to spook over something that never takes place. We've taken care of the other trouble makers and we can do the same with Ellerson. Which reminds me. You see anything more of Buck Devlin?'

Pelly shook his head. 'He's around somewhere, trying to get his nerve back.'

Ackerman's nod was short. 'When Smiley Slade shows tonight, we'll talk things over. Maybe, if we put enough ante on the line, Smiley will make a try for Ellerson with that knife of his. In the meantime, you go hang around Duncan's layout a little and see if you can get any line on what they could be up to.'

Leaving the Lucky Lode, Jack Pelly's wariness was really spurring him. All too plainly, things were becoming shaky. Big and confident talk by Ackerman did not hide the fact that he was hitting the bottle overtime. Which meant that deep down he was badly worried. Also he had hinted of a loss of confidence in Al Rindler as the big gun threat they'd been depending on – while Rindler himself, instead of showing his usual smooth, deadly confidence, was so edgy he seemed ready to explode in any direction at any time. Certainly, things were not as they had been a few days ago.

In the deal Duke Ackerman had been putting across on this camp of Rawhide Creek, a strong element of risk was bound to exist. In this instance the stakes were rich enough to justify the risk. Only up to a point, however, as it was a setup that could last only so long. There was bound to come a time when a smart man, aware of all the signs, knew the deal was playing out and that the edge of safety had become too thin to ignore. Satisfied with his share of the loot, he took it and headed fast and far to newer and safer fields of action. That was what his instinct for personal survival was telling Jack Pelly. The time for him to move was – now ...!

Trouble was, his share was in that squat, ugly safe of Duke Ackerman's and he wasn't about to leave without it. In spite of all the ominous signs, Ackerman was still insisting on staying, hungry for more gold and blinded by it. Furthermore, as he had told Smiley Slade out at the cabin, there was no guarantee that Ackerman would come across with their full share when they asked for it. Therefore, decided Pelly, if he was to make certain of his share before taking off on that fast, long ride, it was something he'd have to make sure of by himself. As this fact shaped up stronger and stronger in Jack Pelly's mind, a reckless excitement entirely foreign to his usual cautious, coldly calculated approach to any business of this sort, came from nowhere to grip him. He had no idea how much gold was really in Ackerman's safe, but one thing was sure. There had to be a lot of it – just a hell of a lot. And if he was to go this thing alone, why be satisfied with just his share – why not collect a good part of the rest of it? Sure – why not ...?

What did he really owe Duke Ackerman, or Al Rindler, or any of them, for that matter? Nothing. Not a damned thing. It had been from the first and still was, strictly a dog-eat-dog game. You might band together to make the whole thing workable, but when the chips were down you looked out for number one, any and all the time. With these thoughts turning over and over in his mind, Jack Pelly crossed to the edge of the camp where his cabin and horse shed stood. Quite suddenly, concern for that horse became very important. It had already covered a considerable distance this day, but a good feeding and several hours of rest should have it ready and able to get him across the summit to Chinese Flat by daylight tomorrow. There he could pick up a fresh horse or, if the timing was right, catch the narrow gauge train on its trip out of the hills. After that ...? Why the whole, big wide world!

He stuffed the horse's manger with all the wild timothy hay it would hold, added a double ration of oats, and while the horse fed hungrily, curried and brushed it down. After which he checked all his gear carefully before flattening out on his bunk to figure the necessary moves ahead.

As the afternoon wore on a greyness filled the sky and dimmed the sun. A raw wind began to gust out of the hills and along the creek flats, and over the loftier summits a boil of clouds massed and darkened. Somewhere beyond the clouds thunder tumbled and growled its approaching threat. Shortly before dusk the first real flare of lightning hissed a ripping way across the world, closer thunder blasted, and then a curtain of chill, late rain began slanting down.

Drawn by the rush of this, Jack Pelly roused and came to the door of his cabin, to look out and exult at the darkening, dripping world. This was all to the good. This might mean wet, cold miserable miles throughout an all-night ride, but it could also hinder and discourage any pursuit. So let it storm!

Dodging the first rush of the rain, Cleve Ellerson sought Scotty Duncan's quarters, built up a fire, rolled a smoke and considered his own plan of action. No part of what lay ahead would be easy. Respecting Scotty's wishes he would, so far as was possible, avoid any open gun play. At the same time he was realistic enough to doubt the possibility of this. For these were ruthless, desperate men he'd be facing, who had already killed and would kill again without compunction should they see it as a need for their own welfare.

He had his first move planned. Earlier, while watching a freight outfit unload a small mountain of barreled flour and other supplies at Peter Yost's store, he saw Jack Pelly cross from the Lucky Lode to his cabin. To have gathered Pelly in then would have meant marching him through camp at the point of a gun, which was certain to be seen and start talk that could reach and warn Duke Ackerman. Night was the time for his business, so night it would be.

Scotty Duncan came stamping in, swearing softly, whipping the wetness from his hat before tossing it into a corner. He doffed his coat and backed up to the stove grumbling, hands spread behind him.

'Damn the rain! Had enough of it last winter. Now that it's spring, I want it to stay spring. What luck did you have?'

'You'll have a customer tonight,' Ellerson promised. 'Got your lockup ready?'

'Ready and empty. Who you going after first?'

'Jack Pelly.'

Scotty considered, then nodded. 'About right. I hope your next will be that rat with the knife, Smiley Slade. I keep remembering Pony Bob McCart and Jake Rivers, and I want the scoundrelly pair who killed them under lock and key. Afterward even more than Duke Ackerman himself, I want to see them hung. By court judgment and authority understand – not by any lynch mob.'

Ellerson smiled faintly. 'What difference does it make who puts the rope around their necks – just so it is there?'

Scotty scrubbed a hand across his face. 'Knew damned well you were going to ask that. No difference, I guess. Only one way is legitimate and the other isn't.'

Ellerson smiled again. 'Everywhere I went out there, I was trailed. Always old Lafe Kenna was loafing along, trying to act and look innocent. You set him after me, didn't you – somebody to watch my back?'

'What if I did?' grunted Scotty testily. 'You're not so good you can take on the whole damn world alone.'

Ellerson's smile became a dry chuckle. 'Scotty, you're an old fraud. You scowl and grumble and act grizzly bear tough, but deep down you're really a gentle soul.'

Scotty grinned sheepishly. 'Make it that I try to be a

decent human being. Yes, I sent Kenna after you. I figured he'd be less noticeable than any. Asked him if he'd ever handled a gun and he said he had, plenty of times. You should have seen him when I handed him a gun and told him to watch your back. I swear the old cuss grew a foot and turned twenty years younger, right before my eyes. Damned if he didn't look like a first class fighting man, instead of a whiskey-soaked old bum.'

'That part's fine,' Ellerson said. 'But I don't want anybody hurt on my account.'

'You're too damned proud,' accused Scotty bluntly. 'Other folks can take a hand in this, too.'

Lightning flickered at the window and thunder belted the drenched world. Scotty swore again. 'I got Tom Searchy coming in from Chinese Flat with a *double* hitch freight rig, which is mean enough on that grade when it's dry. Now, along with the dark and a road turned to slippery mud and the team probably edgy from the storm – well, any man skinning a freight outfit under those conditions is sure earning his wages.' Scotty retrieved his hat and coat and headed outside. 'See you at supper.'

Later, when Ellerson and Scotty turned in at Jim Oliver's place, the storm had let up slightly and Scotty was in better humor because Tom Searchy was safely in with his freight rig. Behind the counter of the eating house, Holly Yarnell was plainly hurried and tired, but she still had a welcoming smile for them.

'Sure gravels me to see how that fine girl and Mrs. Oliver have to work to keep things going while Jim Oliver is laid up,' Scotty growled. 'All because of Duke Ackerman and his damn crowd. It's something I keep remembering.'

'Just so,' Ellerson agreed quietly.

When they were again back in quarters, Ellerson

looked Scotty sternly in the eye. 'One thing I want to get straight. If I'm to do this, I must handle it my way. If everything comes off quiet, which I hope is so, that will be fine. If not, and I have to throw a gun, I'll throw it for keeps. Because this is a mean crowd we're up against and I don't want my hands tied with any orders that could get me killed!'

Scotty measured him carefully, then nodded. 'Whatever you have to do, Cleve – do it!'

In his cabin, as full dark came down, Jack Pelly made his preparations. By lantern light he cooked and ate a solid meal. He made a frugal pack of personal belongings, carried it and his rifle out to the shed. He cinched his saddle on his horse, tied the pack behind the cantle and slung his rifle under the stirrup leather.

Back in the cabin again he lifted a slicker off a wall peg, slit the bottom of the left hand pocket, donned the slicker, thrust his hand through the slit pocket, gripped the yoke of a pair of saddlebags and lifted these until they were fully hidden under the long skirt of his slicker. Held so, they showed no betraying bulk.

Caught up more and more with heady, greedy excitement, he put out the lantern and stepped into an outside world that was wild and black and boisterous with wind and water as the storm again bore down with all its weight. Lightning scorched the world with a leprous glow and thunder pounded out its mighty diapason. Better and better, Pelly exulted. The Lucky Lode would be crowded with miners seeking more warmth and better shelter than their own sketchy quarters could afford. All of which was in his favor.

The deadfall was crowded, all right. It was jammed to the doors. A thick gauze of tobacco smoke dimmed the lights and the air was heavy with wet and earthy odors and the sound of occupancy was a solid growl. Pelly had his careful look around, Placing certain men, in particular Al Rindler, who was at his usual post of faro table lookout, with play heavy enough to hold him safely there for some time. The tinhorn, Carmody, faced a circle of filled chairs at the poker table. Tug Morley, wearing a hat that partially hid the bandage on his head, and looking wan and surly, was behind the bar helping Riordan pour more and more whiskey against the wet and chill of clamoring men.

Like himself, Pelly noted that most of the miners wore slickers which gave them a bulky, formless look. All of which was another aid to him. As he worked a way toward the back room, Tug Morley caught his eyes, pulled him over with a glance and put out a full bottle.

'If you're going in to see Duke, take this with you. He spilled the one he had and I haven't had time to get him another.'

Pelly nodded, taking the bottle. At the door of the rear room he paused for another wary look around. No one was paying him any attention. He tucked the bottle under his arm, opened the door and pushed through, closing it quickly behind him. From his chair behind the table, Duke Ackerman lunged half erect, cursing, a gun ready in his fist.

'God damn it – why can't you people learn to knock? Oh – it's you …!'

'Sure,' Pelly nodded smoothly, setting the bottle on the table. 'Tug Morley said to bring this in. Why the gun? What you so jumpy about?'

Beyond the room's single window lightning's evil glow flickered and the black world overhead exploded with a crash of thunder that shook the very walls.

'That's what does it,' Ackerman exclaimed. 'That damned stuff. Never could feel comfortable with it going on. Sounds like the world breaking up. Made me spill my other bottle.'

He laid his gun aside and began opening the new bottle. Watching the driven urgency with which Ackerman wrestled with the cork of his fresh bottle, Jack Pelly knew a quick, deep contempt. Duke Ackerman was no part of the man he had once been, and he knew for sure his own decision to pull out now had been a wise one. On this thought, Pelly lifted his gun from under his slicker, pushed it level and thumbed back the hammer.

The click of the gun's lock penetrated Ackerman's absorption and brought his head swiftly up. For a moment he stared in shocked disbelief before letting the bottle drop and starting a reaching hand toward the gun at his elbow. He froze at Pelly's bleak warning.

'Touch it and you're dead, Duke! Get over to that safe and open it. I'm leaving this damn camp and I want my share of the take. Hear me now. Don't touch that gun–!'

Thunder again belted the world and as the retreated echoes rumbled off into infinity, Pelly laughed thinly. 'With all those big guns going off, who's to hear this one if I have to pull the trigger? I'm saying it just once more, Duke. Get over to that safe and open it!'

Black, caustic rage swelled Duke Ackerman's throat, congested his cheeks, made his eyes twin bulges of wickedness, even made him slur his words.

'You dirty, double crossing …!?'

Pelly leaned, jammed the muzzle of his gun fairly against Ackerman's mouth, cutting his lips, driving back the rest of his scalding words.

'The safe,' Pelly repeated remorselessly. 'Get over there and open it and lay out what is mine …!'

Ackerman argued no longer. He lurched heavily to his feet, crossed the room and dropped on one knee before the safe, having further say as he worked at the lock.

'You're a damn fool, Pelly. All you had to do was ask for yours decent and I'd have handed it to you. You got no cause to put a gun on me and treat me this way. It's likely you'll come to wish you hadn't!'

He swung back the heavy door, reached for one of the fat buckskin pokes stacked inside. That was when Pelly clipped him above the ear with the heavy barrel of his gun. Ackerman grunted, fell back and half down, where he swayed, dazed and hurt. Pelly hit him again, this time with a full, sweeping blow. Knocked senseless, Ackerman went completely over, a heavy, inert hulk.

For one wild, pulsing moment, stung with a sudden sense of power, Jack Pelly knew the urge to finish things with a bullet at this close range. But the old, sly caution held him back. Enough was enough. The thing to do now was get clear, and quickly. He worked fast, stuffing gold pokes into his saddle bags. They were not nearly big enough to hold all that was in the safe and when they were crammed and buckled up tight, he had all the weight he wanted to carry with one hand. He crouched, got the saddlebags up under his slicker, hand locked round the leather yoke. Pocketing his gun he moved to the door, edged through, closed it carefully and moved toward the street door, tossing curt words to Tug Morley beyond the bar.

'Duke wants some stuff from Yost's store. And in this damn weather …!'

Morley nodded and poured another drink for an insistent miner. Under Pelly's slicker the saddlebags were a solid, dragging weight, so heavy he had to get out of sight before he dropped it. By the time he reached the street his jaw was set with strain, but once in night's blackness he was able to rest a moment. After which he got the bags across his shoulder and headed for his cabin, exulting with every step. Why hell – it had been easy – almost too easy. Now, all he had to do was hit the saddle and ride …

Just about the time Jack Pelly was moving into Duke Ackerman's office, Cleve Ellerson left Scotty Duncan's quarters for Pelly's cabin, finding himself out in the full sweep of a very mean night. A chill rain, driving in at a slant, whipped and stung his cheeks as the unruly wind behind it pulled and tore at him. From time to time pallid lightning flooded the world and thunder hammered out its brawling threat. It was Ellerson's hope to find Pelly holed up in his cabin, it being the kind of night to stay under a sound roof.

When he moved in on the cabin there was no vestige of light or sign of life. The door was unlocked and there was a sense of emptiness about the place. Ellerson drew his gun, pushed open the door and stepped through. Nothing was here but that empty silence, the faint warmth of a cooling stove and the acrid kerosene taint of a lantern lately extinguished. Had the bird, for some reason grown suspicious, already flown? There was one way to find out.

Ellerson circled to the shed out back. Here was animal warmth and a small nicker of equine welcome. Ellerson edged in behind an outstretched exploring hand which presently touched horseflesh and then leather. Hell – this horse was saddled! Searching further, he located the pack behind the saddle cantle and the rifle under the stirrup leather. Somebody was expecting to use this horse, and soon. Jack Pelly wasn't here now, but he would be …

Out of the wind and rain, there was no better place to wait than right here. And what, Ellerson wondered, would Pelly's reaction be when braced? You could never be too sure about such things. A real gun hand of Al Rindler's stripe might cave because he understood the percentages of chance and act accordingly. On the other hand a sly, evasive schemer like Pelly, startled into desperation, could lose his head and go for his gun. So a man had to stay alert to both such possibilities and play each card as it fell.

Shoulder tipped against the shed's doorpost, Ellerson stared out into the night's blackness, searching its substance and mood as best he could. Again and again lightning flickered, followed by the growl and pound of thunder. Between these wilder outbursts fell short intervals of almost breathless pause and quiet as though the storm was gathering strength for another display of cosmic might.

It was during one of these pauses that the first hint of approach reached Ellerson's straining ears. A muffled curse and the slosh and slump of boots hurrying through the mud. Ellerson stepped back into the shed a pace and waited. Abruptly human presence filled the doorway of the shed. Ellerson jammed the muzzle of his gun against a slickered body.

'Hold it – right there!'

Came a bursting exclamation of surprise, the heavy thump of something falling to the shed floor, and then the slickered figure was whirling back into the night. Mindful of his promise to Scotty Duncan, Ellerson lunged in pursuit. In half a step he was falling, tripped by a solid, heavy obstruction that tangled his feet. He was down on his knees when gun flame sliced the outer storm-whipped gloom and, on the heels of the flat, pounding report, lead slashed into the doorpost just above his head. Twice more the gun flame licked out and twice more lead splintered the door post. Maybe the next slug would strike lower …

Holding in his mind's eye the spot of the hostile gun, Ellerson searched the area with three shots of his own. Following the last came a man's choked, disbelieving curse, a fading, half whimpering cry, and after that – nothing.

The obstruction he'd stumbled over was still against Ellerson's leg. Crouching, he ran his hand over it. A pair of saddlebags, tight stuffed, hard and heavy. He shoved his gun under his belt, rubbed his hands dry in his armpits, scratched a sulphur match and by its feeble glow confirmed his guess. Saddlebags, all right, but before he could open them and see what they held, he needed more and bigger light than just a match.

Recalling the kerosene smell in the cabin he hurried around, went inside and by the light of another match located and lit the lantern standing on the cabin table. Carrying this light he was returning to the shed when a call came through the driving rain.

'Hello – the light! Who is it? Lafe Kenna here.'

Ellerson exclaimed his relief. 'Lafe! Come on in, man – come on in!'

Kenna came hurrying and they went into the shed. Ellerson held the lantern high enough to see that Old Lafe was carrying the big Greener shotgun from Scotty's office rack.

'Lot of gun you got there, Lafe.'

Kenna shrugged wet shoulders. 'Figured buckshot might be better in the dark. I heard shootin'. What about it?'

Ellerson explained as they crouched over the saddlebags. The lantern threw its steady glow and the horse, which had stamped and swung and snorted while the guns had rolled their echoes, was now quiet again. With saddlebags open, Lafe Kenna whistled his amazement.

'All these gold pokes! And Jack Pelly had them?'

'Must have been him,' Ellerson said. 'This is his horse, all saddled and ready to go.'

'Where,' Kenna asked, 'is Pelly now?'

'Out yonder somewhere. We'll take a look.'

They found him sprawled on his back in the mud, his upturned face wet and pallid and still in the lantern light. They half carried, half dragged him into the cabin.

TEN

They used Jack Pelly's horse to carry the saddlebags over to Scotty's quarters, and when they had lugged the bags inside and spread the contents, Ellerson told his terse story.

'I gave Pelly his chance, Scotty – but he *would* have it the way it happened. Like all of them, he was desperate. I'd hoped to take him alive. Maybe if I'd stayed down and let him empty his gun and then gone after him …!'

It was Lafe Kenna who spoke up quickly and strongly. 'Oh, sure – if you'd stayed down and Pelly had got you through the head with his next shot – I suppose that would have made everything right? Like hell! You did what you had to do. Pelly had his choice and went for his gun. Maybe he's lucky, at that.'

Scotty made no immediate comment as he sorted through the pokes of gold dust. He hesitated over one of them, staring down at it. It was a fat, tightly stuffed heavy little buckskin sheathed sausage, the leather of it only partly cured as there was still a smudge of hair stubble on it. Now when Scotty did speak, his words were harsh and growling.

'This one – this one right here is the poke Johnny O'Dea sent out on my stage that was held up and my two good men, Pony Bob and Jake Rivers were killed. There can be no further doubt of it. This is proof positive of those responsible.'

He came around them, his blue eyes blazing under shaggy, grizzled brows.

'So you had to gun him? Well, it is good that you did, for it saves honest men the dark chore of hanging him. But he was only one of them and when I've this gold safely put away, we go after the others. We do! This time I go along and there'll be no argument about that!'

Scotty locked the gold in his strong box and led the way out into a night that had suddenly lost its violence. The buffeting wind had blown itself out, the rain had stopped, and a final grumble of thunder was dwindling and distance-dimmed beyond the far peaks. The heavy overcast was breaking up and the world turning brighter as the star gleam filtered through. Men were beginning to leave the Lucky Lode, heading back to their own camps along the creek flats.

Mindful of what the night had already seen, Cleve Ellerson had his final try at dissuading Scotty.

'You don't understand this sort of thing, Scotty. There's a strong Christian streak in you that could make you hesitate to gun down another man, even if it meant saving your own life. You see all things in terms of the law. Now Lafe and me, we're not hobbled that way. We see things strictly in terms of necessity. Oh, we know what Christian feelings are, all right, but we also know how to shed them when it makes sense to.'

Scotty marched stubbornly along. 'I said I'd be with you and I am. Though I would like to take them all in without another shot being fired.'

'A nice thought,' agreed Ellerson dryly. 'But to do that we'd have to get the drop on them, particularly on Duke Ackerman. He's the boss, the head man. If we make him cave, the rest might follow – but I wouldn't count on it.'

'How,' asked Lafe Kenna, 'can we get at him first?'

'There's a back window, as I remember. You go around there. At the right time you knock a hole in that window and shoved the muzzle of the Greener through. The business end of that weapon could be a powerful persuader. Scotty goes with you and does the talking. They might listen to him, knowing he's speaking for all the decent people in camp. In any event, it's all a gamble, of course.'

Tramping along, Scotty considered. 'You might have something there. How do we know anybody will be in the back room?'

'Ackerman's certain to be. If nobody's there, Lafe can come on through the window and get the drop on the barroom from in back. I'll be around front. We'll have them between us.'

Scotty thought on this for another stride or two before nodding agreement. 'Very well, we'll try it. But you give us time to make Ackerman see reason before you do anything.'

In the back room of the Lucky Lode, Duke Ackerman was regaining his stunned senses through a punishing miasma of physical and mind blurring pain. From the floor he made it first to his knees and after wavering there for a time, slowly regained his feet by using the open door of the safe for support. Here he fought for balance of mind and body while trying to judge the full extent of his loss. But things were still too fogged for that so he weaved unsteadily over to his chair and fell into it. His gun still lay on the table and he gripped it tightly and held it in his lap. There was a warm wetness on the side of his face and when he felt of this with his free hand his fingers came away stained with crimson. Dark desperation welled up in him. He'd been betrayed by one of his own crew. From here on out he would trust no one. That was it – no one!

From outside, pushing through a group of departing miners, Smiley Slade entered the Lucky Lode. The ride down from the hill cabin had been a chill, storm-whipped one and long before he got here his thoughts had ranged ahead, anticipating the comforts of the Lucky Lode. Whiskey, of course – a lot of it. And maybe, if everything went smoothly, a few hands of poker before the night was done. Now, with the storm breaking, he had tethered his horse, spread his slicker over his saddle and reached eagerly for the brightness and warmth of the deadfall. He had a swift look around before shouldering up to the bar for a couple of big whiskies from Tug Morley's bottle.

'Better!' he exclaimed. 'I was sure lookin' forward to that.' He measured Morley narrowly, wondering at the pallidness of the slack, surly face and the bandaged head. 'What happened to you?'

Morley didn't like the question, but he liked the hard demand in Slade's glance even less, so he mumbled an answer.

'Got buffaloed when I wasn't lookin'. By a bucko named Ellerson.'

Slade's glance sharpened with a quick, deep interest. 'Ellerson! Did you say Ellerson?' He paused to search a racing memory. 'Would that be – Cleve Ellerson?'

'That's the one,' Morley admitted thickly. 'You know him?'

'Knew a Cleve Ellerson once. What's he doin' around here?'

'Workin' for Scotty Duncan and, so far, raising hell in big chunks.'

A growing wariness wiped out Slade's toothy grin as he made further demand. 'Ackerman on hand? I'm supposed to report to him.'

Morley's glance touched the rear door. 'His usual place. Take it easy, though. He's pretty raunchy these days.'

'Which I can understand if he's got Cleve Ellerson spurrin' him,' Slade said. He drained his glass, put it in front of Morley again. 'Make it another, Tug. It was a damned cold, wet ride comin' down out of the hills in that storm. Seen Jack Pelly around?'

'He was in a little while ago. Went out again. Said he was headin' for Yost's store after somethin' Duke wanted. Ain't back yet. Should have been though, by this time.'

Closing in on the Lucky Lode, Cleve Ellerson, Scotty Duncan and Lafe Kenna passed more and more miners heading away from the place. All of which suited Ellerson, for when he entered the dead-fall the fewer men present the better. For he knew with a fatalistic certainty what lay ahead the next time he faced Al Rindler, no matter where or under what conditions. There would be no backing down a second time. The perverted pride that was at once the strength and the weakness of a man like Rindler would have by this time built up a mad fire that only a showdown, gun against gun, could extinguish. For better or worse, Al Rindler would go for it.

Lafe Kenna was equally aware of this, and before heading around back with Scotty Duncan, he dropped a hand on Ellerson's shoulder together with two murmured words.

'Luck, Cleve!'

In the barroom, having spent a long couple of hours without a break on the faro lookout stool, Al Rindler was glad to see the crowd thin out and play slacken. He was gripped with the odd, disturbed feeling that he had lost touch with some of the business of the evening. He had seen Smiley Slade come in, stop at the bar to drink and talk with Tug Morley. Which was all right, as he knew Duke Ackerman had sent word for Slade to come in and report. But it was Jack Pelly who had Rindler pondering and wondering. Because Pelly had shown up earlier, gone in to see Ackerman, then come out and left and had not come back. It was something to wonder at.

At the bar, Smiley Slade downed his last drink, squared his blocky shoulders against the shock of it, then showed Tug Morely his big toothed grin again. 'Now to go in and cool Duke's fevered brow.'

He went along to the rear door, stepped through, then stopped dead still for a long breath before closing the door behind him. From beyond the table Duke Ackerman stared at him with hot, bitter eyes. Blood ran its crimson track down the side of Ackerman's face and his words bit out savagely.

'And what would you be wanting?'

Raunchy is right, Slade thought, giving back his own curt answer. 'Understood you wanted to see me. Somebody buffalo you, too? Somebody named Ellerson, maybe?'

'Not Ellerson,' Ackerman ground out harshly. 'But Jack Pelly, and may God forever damn his double-crossing soul! Yeah, he buffaloed me. Came in here saying he was pulling out, leaving the camp. Threw a gun on me and made me open the safe. While I'm getting his share for him he clubbed me down, knocked me cold. He's long gone now, and from all I can tell, he took a lot more with him than he had coming.'

Ever the suspicious one, seeing no good in any other man because he possessed none himself, Smiley Slade picked Ackerman's explanation apart. If Pelly had to throw a gun to make Ackerman come across, what would he have to do to make sure of getting his share?

He glanced at the safe. The door still swung open. In that moment Smiley Slade made the ruthless decision of a thoroughly greedy, savage, avaricious man. His hand went under his coat and came out gripping the hilt of his favorite weapon, a heavy, gleaming Bowie knife. He stepped toward the table with both vocal and physical threat.

'Ackerman, I've used this knife for you,' he said wickedly. 'Now I'll use it on you unless you do as I say. If you could count out Jack Pelly's share, you can count out mine – and make it plenty. Get at it!'

Duke Ackerman looked at the knife, looked at the burly threat of the man behind it. He came slightly forward in his chair, laughing a little wildly.

'Two of them!' he exclaimed. 'First Pelly. Now this damn knife-wielding dog. So much for honor among thieves!'

He laughed again, tipped the muzzle of his gun above the edge of the table and shot Smiley Slade through the heart.

In the barroom, with the faro table momentarily empty of play, Al Rindler slid off the lookout stool, stretched and flexed his arms and shoulders, then went dead still at the hard, flat pound of gun report in the back room. All evening, together with everyone else, he had listened to massive, cosmic shots of thunder reverberating across the world. But it was not thunder this time – this was man-made gun talk. Drawing his own weapon, Rindler rushed to the rear door, slammed it open and went through in a half crouch like a feline about to spring.

On the floor in front of him, Smiley Slade was sprawled. Just beyond his outstretched hand the burnished steel of a heavy knife glittered in the lamp light. Behind the table Duke Ackerman was hunched in his chair, blood on the side of his face, his protuberant eyes wild and sick. Sight of the knife and the line of blood on Ackerman's face gave Rindler pause, exclaiming:

'What the hell, Duke – he cut you?'

'Was set to, the dirty whelp! Now if I could only put Jack Pelly alongside of him – and just as dead, I wouldn't mind the gold Pelly got away with.'

'Gold! Pelly got away with what gold …?'

'Take a look at the safe,' Ackerman said. 'Pelly came in and put his gun on me. Made me open the safe. Then he gunwhipped me. You knew about how much we had in the safe. See how much he got away with.'

Rindler looked at Ackerman, looked at the dead man on the floor, then looked at the safe. He put his gun away and was moving toward the safe when glass crashed from the window and the awesome muzzle of the big Greener shotgun drove through. Came also a harsh call in an unmistakable burring Scottish brogue.

'This is Scotty Duncan. I declare you under arrest. Drop your guns!'

Duke Ackerman made no move, for or against. Reaction had him by the throat and his world was all on end. Not so with Al Rindler. As fast and cat-like as he had entered he now whipped back in to the barroom, again drawing his gun.

Only a little way from the street door of the Lucky Lode when the shot sounded, Cleve Ellerson moved swiftly in, his glance raking the room, Behind the bar, Riordan and Tug Morley were swung around, staring toward the rear. At the poker table, Carmody and four startled miners were pulled up high in their chairs, watching the same direction. And now it was Al Rindler, gun in hand, spinning into sight through the rear door.

His own gun ready, Ellerson hit Rindler with cold, mocking challenge.

'This time, Al – *this time!* You quitting again, or going for it?'

Al Rindler was a man whip-sawed and driven. So much had come at him in swift, fierce succession. The shot that killed Smiley Slade. Sight of Slade sprawled and dead and of Ackerman's bloody face and wild, sick eyes. Ackerman's short explanation and the mockery of the open safe. Then it was the crash of window glass and the threat of a gaping shotgun muzzle and Scotty Duncan's harsh call. Now it was this, the high figure of Cleve Ellerson facing him, challenging him, pushing him implacably toward the moment of truth …

So much over the space of a few fast ticking moments, and no time now to think or calculate the percentage of chance. No time to do anything but take the final desperate gamble …!

He took it, crouched and venomous. But even as his gun stabbed level, Ellerson's bullet took him, driving into him, beating him back, knocking all coordination out of him. Intolerable pain came flooding and the world went crazy in all degrees of balance and distance. Through fast dimming faculties he glimpsed what seemed to him to be a threatening figure and by pure instinct alone he threw the shot. After that everything left him – pain, light, the hazy world as he dropped into an endless black.

At the inner end of the bar, Tug Morley gave muffled exclamation, staggered back against the bottle shelf, lurched forward again to sprawl head and arms and shoulders on the bar top and then slide slowly off again in a heavy fall. Rindler's lone, half-blind shot had taken him squarely. And so it was that in his final moment of life, Al Rindler, self-proclaimed high priest of the deadly gun, killed his last man.

Ellerson threw a bleak command across the room. 'Riordan – Carmody, stay put! You hear me?'

They heard and did not move. Ellerson went along to the rear door, reaching it just as Lafe Kenna smashed out the rest of the low window and came through it behind the big Greener. In back of him was the anxious, concerned face of Scotty Duncan. Duke Ackerman made no hostile move. He had the dazed, apathetic look of a man whose world had just crumbled before his eyes and who no longer gave a damn. At sight of Ellerson, he roused enough to show a resigned shrug.

'So you were the fastest after all. You had to be or you wouldn't be here if Al Rindler wasn't dead. So …?'

Ellerson's nod was curt. 'That's how it stands.'

'Too bad it wasn't the same with Jack Pelly. He got away with most of my gold.'

'Wrong,' Ellerson said. 'He never got away with anything. He got only as far as his cabin. And he's still there.'

'Be damned!' Ackerman exclaimed slackly. 'Out-smarted himself, did he? Well, knowing how he ended will make it easier to take what's ahead.' He paused, his features twisted, his protuberant eyes blinking as though trying to peer into the future and read what awaited him there. There was apparently nothing there that was comforting, for suddenly he seemed to shrink and shrivel. And his words, meant only for his own ears, ran thin and reedy.

'So Pelly was right, after all. I waited too long – too long!'

They gathered later in Jim Oliver's living room. Ellerson, Scotty Duncan and Peter Yost. Scotty spoke soberly.

'As decent, respectable men we have done that which had to be done. We cannot bring back from the dead the good men who were our friends and comrades. But so far as is possible we can see that the gold recovered from

Ackerman's safe goes out to the kin of these men. It is poor recompense for lost lives, but it is the best we can do. Agreed?'

'Agreed,' Peter Yost said. 'It is the fair and just thing.'

'And Ackerman?' Jim Oliver asked.

'Safe under lock and key,' Scotty told him. 'I have spoken to Toby Stent, a neighbor of Johnny O'Dea. He is a good, reliable man and he will organize a miners' court. Ackerman will be turned over to that court. It will be a court of honest men and their verdict, whatever it is, will be a fair and honest one. We will abide by it.'

They kept it as simple and basic as that and so were soon done. Once more in the street, Ellerson and Scotty headed for quarters. But for the wet earth under foot and the fresh, keen bite of the air, it was as though there had never been a storm. Across the velvet black dome of the heavens the stars were all one great glittering wash, letting down a light that turned night's normal gloom into a silvered glow.

A great stillness held the world, as if the storm with its thunder had used up all the elements of sound. Scotty Duncan was clearing his throat for some remark to Ellerson when Lafe Kenna's strident, concerned call of warning came.

'Heads up, Cleve – heads up! Devlin – over by the trading post! Watch it, boy …!'

In the shadow cast by the loom of the trading post a man's startled curse sounded, and then a gun began to pound. Instantly Ellerson flung away from Scotty, drew his gun, whirled and ran straight in at the point of danger, shooting as he went. That was when the booming voice of the big Greener shotgun wiped out all lesser sound, and as the echo of this ran out against the wondering sky, the world lay still again except for Ellerson's anxious call.

'Lafe, you all right?'

'All right, Devlin's down. He was laying for you, boy.'

Buck Devlin's lank figure was crumpled against the foot of the trading post wall. Lafe Kenna stood over him, the reeking Greener across his arm. While Ellerson went down on one knee for quick examination by match light, Scotty Duncan came hurrying up.

'Devlin – no mistake?'

'No mistake,' Ellerson said, lifting to his feet.

'Hell of a note,' old Lafe Kenna murmured, queerly soft and regretful. 'Yet I had no other choice. He was in the shadow and you were an open target. Why did he have to make this sort of thing necessary? I never liked the man, but I'm sorry it had to be this way.'

Ellerson took him by the arm. 'No regrets, Lafe. Like Jack Pelly, he asked for it. And you stood up straight, Lafe – you stood up plenty straight …!'

ELEVEN

It was a clean-washed, bright and burnished world that greeted Cleve Ellerson when he stepped out into the next morning's sunshine. No vestige of cloud showed anywhere and the air was so clear and fresh it laid a strong flavor on a man's tongue. Yet, great as it was, the morning's goodness could not wipe out the bitter dregs of last night, not when you toted up the results of violence with the stark figures of men still alive and of men now dead. The black hell of it was that you couldn't just walk away from such things and forget them. Life was never that simple. The bad moments always returned and these afterthoughts were almost as bad as the actual affair. They stayed with a man a long time before the healing balm of forgetfulness began its cure. And in total they saddled a man with an outcast's loneliness.

Hardly realizing where his steps were taking him, he knew honest surprise when he found himself at the door of Jim Oliver's eating house. For a time he'd had no desire for breakfast; now he thought of hot coffee with a relish. It was well past the breakfast hour, so the place was empty. Yet, when he sat up to the counter, Holly Yarnell came hurrying immediately with the steaming cup. He looked up at her and it was as it had always been with him and this girl; he saw her neat and crisp and full of beauty. Cradling his cup in both hands, he spoke gravely.

'How did you know I wanted this?'

'Scotty Duncan was in earlier. He said I was to look out for you when you showed up. He said it would help.'

Ellerson's slow nod carried with it the edge of a smile. 'Good man, Scotty. Smart, too. He had it right. So now you just stand there and let me look at you. Helps to thin out the shadows and let in the light.'

Now her eyes were very big and very gentle, and her lips a trifle unsteady. 'Scotty told Jim and Helen and me all about it. Oh, Cleve – it was terrible, wasn't it? It had to be …!'

He drank of his coffee, set the cup slowly down. 'That's one word for it,' he agreed. 'There's another which explains why a man can continue to live with it. Necessity – that's it, necessity. I've found that though a man burdens himself with a lot of doubts, he generally ends up doing what he has to do. It was that way with me last night. Something I had to do. Because there can come a time when a man finds he owes a debt to the decent world and that there's no real peace left for him until he squares that debt. I tried to square mine last night. If I did, then the scars I gathered are worthwhile.'

Her eyes began to fill. 'D – darn it!' she gulped. 'In a minute, talking that way, you'll have me bawling. I've a notion not to get you any breakfast.'

She scurried off, but was soon back, bearing a tray. She put hot food before him, with more coffee and a cup of the same for herself. Then she came around the end of the counter and took a seat beside him, speaking brightly.

'Remember the last time I sat with you while you ate? Up on the stage coming over the summit?'

'I haven't forgotten a single second of it. And never will.'

Color rouged her cheeks and her eyes sparkled. 'Now that you feel your debt has been paid, what do you expect to do?'

He considered thoughtfully. 'Before we go into that, here is what I want you to do. I want you to look me over and see if I appear any different than I did at this time yesterday.'

She studied him gravely. 'What a strange question. Why do you ask it?'

'It's something I've wondered about. Whether going through a deal like that one last night can add something to a man or take something away, and leave a difference in him that you can tell just by looking at him. Does a gun like mine leave a brand on a man?'

'Of course not,' Holly said swiftly. 'I'll have you know, Mister Cleve Ellerson, that you are sitting with, talking to, and looking at the youngest daughter of a former sheriff, and one of the best. No kinder, more gentle man than my father ever lived, yet he could be terrible when he had to. And when he would come home, full of darkness, my mother would warm and comfort him with understanding until he was a whole man again. Rightness never leaves a stain – and last night you were right!'

He felt a sense of lightness go through him. 'Sometimes,' he said gently, 'a man's sheer luck can take his breath away. You asked me what I intended to do, now that I've paid my debt. The answer is that it depends on several things.'

'Such as,' she nudged quickly.

'The important one is you,' he returned steadily. 'What you do and say will tell it all – whether I ride on – or I stay.'

She couldn't avoid the clear demand in his glance and she did not try to. Her eyes were warm and shining and what he saw dawning in them was a beauty he'd never believed existed anywhere.

'You're going to stay, Cleve,' she told him softly. 'You're going to stay ...!'